"Marry me,

She put her hand o
heart, Noah. I can fe
steady in there."

"What is that supposed to mean?"

"It means I know what I want now, after years
of throwing myself wildly into all kinds of iffy
situations." Just like a woman. She knew what she
wanted, but she failed to share it with him.

"And what, exactly, is it that you want, Alice?"

"I want it all. I'll have nothing less. I want everything.
Not only your strength and protection, your fidelity
and your hot body. Not only your brilliant brain and
great sense of humor and your otherworldly way
with my horses. I want your heart, too. And I know
I don't have that yet. And until I do, I won't say yes
to you."

* * *

The Bravo Royales:
When it comes to love, Bravos rule!

Dear Reader,

I love a man who knows what he wants and goes after it. Noah Cordell is that kind of guy. Charming, killer hot and something of a player, Noah started with nothing and he's come a long way.

Professional horse breeder Alice Bravo-Calabretti, Princess of Montedoro, is at a crossroads in her life. She's always been the adventurous one in her family, the impetuous, unpredictable one. But just recently, an innocent evening of fun went a little too far and turned into a major tabloid scandal. Since then, Alice has sworn to behave in a more princesslike manner. She's been keeping a low profile and reexamining what she wants out of life.

Enter Noah, who wants Alice.

He's willing to offer her everything—except for his shadowed heart. But Alice won't be satisfied with his strength and protection, his fidelity, his hot body and half of everything he owns. She wants more from him than his "brilliant brain and great sense of humor and his otherworldly way with her horses."

Alice will settle for nothing less than true love. And so, in the process of relentlessly pursuing what he wants, Noah just might end up getting what he really needs.

Happy reading, everyone,

Christine

a Princess

———

Christine Rimmer

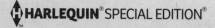
HARLEQUIN® SPECIAL EDITION®

Recycling programs
for this product may
not exist in your area.

ISBN-13: 978-0-373-65776-6

HOW TO MARRY A PRINCESS

Copyright © 2013 by Christine Rimmer

Printed in U.S.A.

™ www.Harlequin.com

CHRISTINE RIMMER

came to her profession the long way around. Before settling down to write about the magic of romance, she'd been everything from an actress to a salesclerk to a waitress. Now that she's finally found work that suits her perfectly, she insists she never had a problem keeping a job—she was merely gaining "life experience" for her future as a novelist. Christine is grateful not only for the joy she finds in writing, but for what waits when the day's work is through: a man she loves who loves her right back, and the privilege of watching their children grow and change day to day. She lives with her family in Oregon. Visit Christine at www.christinerimmer.com.

For MSR,
always.

Chapter One

On the first Wednesday in September, temptation came looking for Alice Bravo-Calabretti.

And she'd been doing so well, too. For more than two weeks, she'd kept her promise to herself. She'd maintained a low profile and carried herself with dignity. She'd accepted no dares and avoided situations where she might be tempted to go too far.

It hadn't been all that difficult. She'd spent her days with her beloved horses and her nights at home. Temptation, it seemed, presented no problem when she made sure there was none.

And then came that fateful Wednesday.

It happened in the stables well before dawn. Alice was tacking up one of the mares, Yasmine, for an early-morning ride. She'd just placed the saddle well forward on the mare's sleek back when she heard a rustling sound in the deserted stable behind her.

Yasmine twitched her tail and whickered softly, her distinctive iridescent coat shimmering even in the dim light provided by the single caged bulb suspended over the stall. A glance into the shadows and Alice registered the source of the unexpected noise.

Over near the arched door that led into the courtyard, a stable hand was pushing a broom. He was no one she recognized, which she found somewhat odd. The palace stables were a second home to her. Alice knew every groom by name. He must be new.

Gilbert, the head groom, came in from the dark yard. He said something to the man with the broom. The man laughed low. Gilbert chuckled, too. Apparently the head groom liked the new man.

With a shrug, Alice gave the beautiful mare a comforting pat and finished tacking up. She was leading Yazzy out of the stall when she saw that Gilbert had gone. The stable hand remained. He'd set his broom aside and lounged against the wall by the door to the courtyard.

As she approached, the man straightened from the wall and gave her a slow nod. "Your Highness." His voice was deep and rather stirring, his attitude both ironic and confident. She recognized his accent instantly: American.

Alice had nothing against Americans. Her father was one after all. And yet...

As a rule, the grooms were Montedoran by birth— and diffident by nature. This fellow was simply not the sort Gilbert usually hired.

The groom raised his golden head. Blue eyes met hers. She saw mischief in those eyes and her heart beat faster.

Temptation. Oh, yes.

Down, girl. Get a grip.

So what if the new groom was hot? So what if just a glance from him had her thinking of how boring her life had become lately, had her imagining all kinds of inappropriate activities she might indulge in with him?

Nothing inappropriate is happening here, she reminded herself staunchly.

And then, in an attempt to appear stern and formidable, she drew her shoulders back and gave the man a slow once-over. He wore a disreputable sweatshirt with the sleeves ripped off, old jeans and older Western boots.

Hot. Definitely. Tall and fit, with a scruff of bronze beard on his lean cheeks. She wondered briefly why Gilbert hadn't required him to dress in the brown trousers, collared shirt and paddock boots worn by the rest of the stable staff.

He stepped forward and her thoughts flew off in all directions. "Such a beautiful girl," he said in a tender tone—to the mare. Alice stared, bemused, as he stroked Yazzy's long, sleek face.

Like most of her ancient hotblood breed, Yasmine was a fiercely loyal, sensitive animal. She gave her trust and affection to very few. But the bold and handsome American worked a certain magic on the golden mare. Yazzy nuzzled him and nickered fondly as he petted her.

Alice permitted his attentions to the horse. If Yazzy didn't mind, neither did she. And watching him with the mare, she began to understand why Gilbert had hired him. He had a way with horses. Plus, judging by his tattered clothing, the fellow probably needed the work. The kindhearted head groom must have taken pity on him.

Finally, the new man stepped back. "Have a nice ride, ma'am." The words were perfectly mundane, the tone pleasant and deferential. *Ma'am* was the proper form of address.

The look in his eyes, though?

Anything but proper. Far from deferential.

"Thank you. I shall." She led the mare out into the gray light of coming dawn.

* * *

The new groom had disappeared when Alice returned from her morning ride. That didn't surprise her. The grooms were often needed outside the stables.

Her country, the principality of Montedoro, was a tiny slice of paradise overlooking the Mediterranean on the Côte d'Azur. The French border lay less than two kilometers from the stables and her family owned a chain of paddocks and pastures in the nearby French countryside. A stable hand might be required to exercise the horses in some far pasture or help with cleanup or fence repair at one of the paddocks.

And honestly, what did it matter to her where the handsome American had gone off to? He was nothing to her. She resisted the urge to ask Gilbert about him and reminded herself that becoming overly curious about one of the grooms was exactly the sort of self-indulgence she couldn't permit herself anymore.

Not after the Glasgow episode.

Her face flamed just thinking about it.

And she *needed* to think about it. She needed to keep her humiliation firmly in mind in order to never allow herself to indulge in such unacceptable behavior again.

Like most of her escapades, it had begun so innocently.

On a whim, she'd decided to visit Blair Castle for the International Horse Trials and Country Fair. She'd flown to Perth the week before the trials thinking she would spend a few days touring Scotland.

She'd never made it to Blair Castle. She'd met up with some friends in Perth and driven with them down to Glasgow. Such fun, a little pub hopping. They'd found this one lovely, rowdy pub and it was karaoke night.

Alice had enjoyed a pint or two more than she should have. Her bodyguard, huge, sweet old Altus, had caught her eye more than once and given her *the look*—the one meant to warn her that she was going too far, the one that rarely did any good.

As usual, she'd ignored *the look*. Repeatedly. And then, somehow, there she was up on the stage singing that Katy Perry song, "I Kissed a Girl." At the time, it had seemed like harmless fun. She'd thrown herself into her performance and acted out the lyrics.

Pictures of her soul-kissing that cute Glaswegian barmaid with her skirt hiked up and her top halfway off had been all over the scandal sheets. The paparazzi had had a field day. Her mother, the sovereign princess, had not been amused.

And after that, Alice had sworn to herself that she would do better from now on—which definitely meant steering clear of brash, scruffy American stable hands who made her pulse race.

The next morning, Thursday, the new groom appeared again. He was there, busy with his broom, when she entered the stables at five. The sight of him, in the same disreputable jeans and torn sweatshirt as the day before, caused a thoroughly annoying flutter in her solar plexus, as well as a definite feeling of breathlessness.

To cover her absurd excitement over seeing him again, she said, "Excuse me," in a snooty abovestairs-at-Downton-Abbey tone that she instantly regretted, a tone that had her wondering if she might be trying *too* hard to behave. "I didn't catch your name."

He stopped sweeping. "Noah. Ma'am."

"Ah. Well. Noah…" She was suddenly as tongue-tied

as a preteen shaking hands with Justin Bieber. Ridiculous. Completely ridiculous. "Would you saddle Kajar for me, please?" She gave a vague wave of her hand toward the stall where the gray gelding waited. As a rule, she personally tacked up any horse she rode. It helped her read the horse's mood and condition and built on the bond she established with each of the animals in her care.

But once she'd opened her mouth, she'd had to come up with a logical excuse for talking to him.

And she was curious. Would he work the same magic, establish the same instant comfortable rapport with Kajar as he had with Yazzy?

The groom—Noah—set aside his broom and went to work. Kajar stood patiently under his firm, calm hands. Noah praised the horse as he worked, calling him fine and handsome and good. The gelding gave no trouble through the process. On the contrary. Twice Kajar turned his long, graceful neck to whicker at Noah as though in approval and affection.

Once the job was done, the groom led the horse from the stall and passed Alice the reins. His long fingers whispered across her gloved palm and were gone. For a moment she caught the scent of his clean, healthy skin. He wore a light aftershave. It smelled of citrus, of sun and cedar trees.

She should have said, "Thank you," and led the horse out to ride. But he drew her so strongly. She found herself instigating an actual conversation. "You're not Montedoran."

"How did you guess?" Softly. With humor and a nice touch of irony.

"You're American."

"That's right." He looked at her steadily, those eyes

of his so blue they seemed almost otherworldly. "I grew up in California, in Los Angeles. In Silver Lake and East L.A." He was watching her in that way he had: with total concentration. A wry smile stretched the corners of his mouth. "You have no idea where Silver Lake is, or East L.A., do you? Ma'am." He was teasing her.

She felt a prickle of annoyance, which only increased her interest in him. "I have a basic understanding, yes. I've been to Southern California. I have a second cousin there. He and his family live in Bel Air."

"Bel Air is a long way from East L.A."

She leaned into Kajar, cupping her hand to his far cheek, resting her head against his long, fine neck. The gelding didn't object, only made a soft snuffling sound. "A long distance, you mean?"

One strong shoulder lifted in a shrug. "It's not so far in miles. However, Bel Air has some of the priciest real estate in the world—kind of like here in Montedoro. East L.A.? Not so much."

She didn't want to talk about real estate. Or class differences. And she needed to be on her way. She went as far as to stop leaning on the horse—but then, what do you know? She opened her mouth and another question popped out. "Do your parents still live there?"

"No. My father was killed working construction when I was twelve. My mother died of the flu when I was twenty-one."

Sympathy for him moved within her, twining with the excitement she felt at his nearness. Kajar tossed his head. She turned to the gelding, reaching up to stroke his elegant face, settling him. And then she said to Noah, "That is too sad."

"It is what it is."

She faced the groom fully again. "It must have been horrible for you."

"I learned to depend on myself."

"Do you have brothers and sisters?"

"A younger sister. Lucy is twenty-three."

She wanted to ask *his* age—but somehow that seemed such an intimate question. There were fine lines at the corners of his eyes. He had to be at least thirty. "What brings you to Montedoro?"

He seemed faintly amused. "You're full of questions, Your Highness."

She answered honestly. "It's true. I'm being very nosy." *And it's time for me to go.* But she didn't go. She kept right on being as nosy as before. "How long have you been here, in my country?"

"Not long at all."

"Do you plan to stay on?"

"That depends...."

"On?"

He didn't answer, only held her gaze.

She felt the loveliest, most effervescent sensation. Like champagne sliding, cool and fizzy, down her throat. "You love horses."

"Yes, I do. And you're wondering how a guy from East L.A. learned to handle horses...."

Tell him that you really do have to go. "I have been wondering exactly that."

"When I was eighteen, I went to work for a man who owned a horse ranch in the Santa Monica Mountains. He taught me a lot. And I learned fast. He kept warm bloods. Hanoverians and Morgans, mostly."

"Excellent breeds." She nodded in approval. "Strong, steady and handsome. Not nearly so testy and sensitive as an Akhal-Teke." All her horses were Tekes. Akhal-Tekes were called the "heavenly horses," the oldest breed on earth. Originating in the rugged deserts of Turkmenistan and northern Iran, the Teke was swift and temperamental and very tough. Both Genghis Khan and Alexander the Great chose Akhal-Tekes to carry them into battle.

"There is nothing like an Akhal-Teke," he said. "I hope to own one someday."

"An admirable goal."

He chuckled and the sound seemed to slide like a sweet caress across her skin. "Aren't you going to tell me that I'll never be able to afford one?"

"That would be rude. And besides, you seem a very determined sort of person. I would imagine that if you want something strongly enough, you'll find a way to have it." He said nothing, only regarded her steadily through those beautiful eyes. She was struck with the sense that there was much more going on here than she understood. "What is it?" she asked finally, when the silence had stretched thin.

"I *am* determined."

She found herself staring at his mouth. The shape of it—the slight bow of his top lip, the fullness below—was so intriguing. She wondered what it might feel like, that mouth of his touching hers. It would be so very easy to step in close, go on tiptoe and claim a kiss....

Stop. No. Wrong. Exactly the sort of foolish, bold, unprincess-like behavior she was supposed to be avoiding at all costs.

"I…" She was still staring at his lips.

"Yeah?" He moved an inch closer.

She clutched the reins tighter. "…really must be on my way."

He instantly stepped back and she wished that he hadn't—which was not only contrary but completely unacceptable. "Ride safe, ma'am."

She nodded, pressing her lips together to keep them from trembling. Then she clucked her tongue at Kajar and turned for the wide-open stable door.

Once again he was gone when she returned from her ride. That day, she worked with a couple of the yearlings and put one of the show jumpers through his paces. Later she went home to shower and change.

In the afternoon, she met with the planning committee for next year's Grand Champions Tour. Montedoro would host the sixth leg of the tour down at the harbor show grounds in June. Through the endless meeting, she tried very hard not to think of blue eyes, not to remember the deep, stirring sound of a certain voice.

That night, alone in her bed, she dreamed she went riding with Noah. She was on Yasmine and he rode the bay stallion Orion. They stopped in a meadow of wildflowers and talked, though when she woke she couldn't remember a thing they had said.

It was a very tame dream. Not once did they touch, and there was none of the heated tension she had felt when she'd actually been near him. In the dream they laughed together. They were like longtime companions who knew each other well.

She woke Friday morning as usual, long before dawn, feeling edgy and dissatisfied, her mind on the American.

Why? She hardly knew this man. She *didn't* know him. She'd seen him twice and shared one brief conversation with him. He should not have affected her so profoundly.

Then again, there was probably nothing profound about it. He was hot and mysterious, untamed and somehow slightly dangerous. He called to her wild side. She found him madly attractive.

Plus, well, maybe she'd been keeping too much to herself. She wanted to avoid getting wild in the streets, but that didn't mean she couldn't have a life. She'd been sticking *too* close to home. This obsession with Noah was clear proof that she needed to get out more.

And she would get out, starting that very evening with a gala party at the palace, a celebration of her sister Rhiannon's recent marriage to Commandant Marcus Desmarais. It would be lovely. She would enjoy herself. She would dance all night.

She rose and dressed and went to the stables, expecting to see Noah again, unsure whether she *wanted* to see him—or wished that he wouldn't be there.

He wasn't there.

And her uncertainty vanished. She *did* want to see him, to hear his voice again, to find out if her response to him was as strong as it had seemed yesterday. As she tacked up the black mare Prizma, she was alert every moment for the telltale sound of someone entering the stables behind her. But no one came.

She went for her ride, returning to find that he still wasn't there. She almost asked Gilbert about him.

But she felt too foolish and confused—which wasn't like her at all. She was a confident person, always had been. She spoke her mind and had few fears. Yes, she was making a definite effort not to get into situations that might attract the attention of the tabloids and embarrass her family. But that didn't mean she was all tied up in emotional knots. She liked to live expansively, to take chances, to have fun.

She was no shy little virgin afraid to ask a few questions about a man who interested her.

The problem was…

Wait a minute. There *was* no problem. She'd met a man and found him attractive. She might or might not see him again. If she ever did get something going with him, well, it *could* be a bit awkward. She was a princess of Montedoro and he was a penniless American from a place called East Los Angeles.

They didn't exactly have a whole lot in common.

Except that they did. She *was* half American after all. And they both loved horses. And she had so enjoyed talking with him. Plus, he was very easy on the eyes….

She'd made way too much of this and she was stopping that right now. He was only a man she found intriguing. She might see him again.

And she might not. The world would go on turning however things worked out.

At six o'clock, Alice returned to her villa on a steep street in the ward of Monagalla, not far from the palace. Her housekeeper, Michelle Thierry, met her at the front door.

"I thought you'd never get back," the housekeeper chided. "Have you forgotten your sister's party?"

"Of course not. Relax. There's plenty of time."

"You're to be there at eight, you said," Michelle accused.

"Oh, come on. It's definitely doable."

Michelle wrinkled her nose. "What *have* you stepped in?"

"I work all day with horses. Take a guess."

The housekeeper waved her hands. "Don't just stand there. Get out of those boots and come inside. We'll have to hurry. There's so much to do...."

"You are way too bossy."

Michelle granted her a smug smile. "But you couldn't get along without me."

It was only the truth.

In her late forties, Michelle was a wonder. She not only took excellent care of the villa but also cooked beautiful meals and played lady's maid with skill and flair. Michelle loved her work and had impeccable taste. Alice knew she was lucky to have her.

Laughing, she perched on the step and took off her boots, which the housekeeper instantly whisked from her hands.

"The bath," Michelle commanded, waving a soiled boot. "Immediately."

Alice had her bath, did her hair and makeup, put on the red silk-taffeta Oscar de la Renta that Michelle had chosen for her and then sat impatiently, fully dressed except for her shoes, while Michelle repaired her manicure and pedicure and clucked over her for not taking proper care of her hands.

The car was waiting outside when she left the villa at ten of eight. The drive up to Cap Royale, the bluff overlooking the Mediterranean on which the Prince's Palace sprawled in all its white stone glory, should have taken only a few minutes. But the streets were packed with limousines on their way to the party. Alice could have walked it faster—and at one time, she would have simply told the driver to pull over and let her out. But no. The goal was to be more dignified, less of a wild child. She stayed in her limo like everyone else. The car finally reached the palace at 8:28 p.m. Hardly late at all, the way Alice saw it. But her mother would think otherwise. Her Sovereign Highness Adrienne expected the members of her family to arrive promptly at important events.

The guests in their gala finery were still streaming in the red-carpeted main entrance. Alice had the driver take her around to a side door where two stern-faced palace guards waited to let in intimate friends and members of the princely family. She gave her light wrap and bag to a servant.

Then she took a series of marble hallways to another exit—the one that led out to the colonnade above the palace gardens. Alice paused at the top of the white stone stairs leading down to the garden.

Below, a giant white silk tent had been erected. Golden light glowed from within the tent, where dinner for three hundred would be served. The palace, the tent, the gardens, the whole of Montedoro—everything seemed ablaze with golden light.

"There you are." Her sister Rhiannon, five months pregnant and glowing with happiness, clutched the frothy tiered skirts of her strapless ivory gown and sailed up the stairs to Alice's side, her growing baby bump leading the way.

Alice adored all four of her sisters, but she and Rhia shared a special bond. They were best friends. "Sorry I'm a little late. The streets are awash in limousines."

The sisters shared a quick hug and kissed the air by each other's cheeks. Rhia whispered, "I'm just glad you're here. I've missed you…." Flashes went off. There were always photographers lurking around, way too many of them at an event like this.

Alice hooked her arm through Rhia's. They turned as

one to face the cameras. "Smile," Alice advised softly, trying not to move her lips. "Show no weakness."

Rhia braced her free hand proudly on the bulge of her tummy and smiled for the cameras. She had a lot to be happy about. For almost a decade she'd struggled to deny her love for Marcus Desmarais. Now, at last, she and her lifetime love were together in the most complete way. Rhia and Marcus had married in a small private ceremony three weeks ago. They'd flown off for a honeymoon in the Caribbean on the same day Alice had made that fateful trip to Scotland.

The party tonight was in lieu of the usual big wedding. The world needed to see how the Bravo-Calabretti family welcomed the new husband of one of their own.

Rhia's groom had been orphaned soon after his birth. He'd started with nothing—and become a fine man, one who'd gone far in spite of his humble beginnings. The party wasn't just for show. The Bravo-Calabrettis did welcome him.

Alice loved that about her family. They judged a man—or a woman—by his or her behavior and accomplishments. Not by an accident of birth or a string of inherited titles. If Alice were to choose a man with nothing, her family would support her in her choice.

Not that she was anywhere close to choosing anyone. Certainly not a bold blue-eyed American she'd only just met and would likely not see again.

She banished the stable hand from her mind—yet again—as Rhia grabbed her hand and pulled her down the curving staircase. They wove their way through the crowd toward the wide-open entrance to the big white tent. Alice spotted her brother Damien, the youngest of the four Bravo-Calabretti princes, entering the tent, his dark head thrown back as he laughed at something the tall golden-haired man beside him had said....

"Allie?" Rhia turned back to her with a puzzled frown.

Alice realized she'd stopped in midstep at the base of the stairs and was staring with her mouth hanging open. Her brother and the other man disappeared inside the tent. She'd only caught the briefest glimpse of the other man from the back. And then from the side, for that split second when he'd turned his head. "It can't be..."

"Allie?" her sister asked again.

"I could have sworn..."

"Are you all right?" A worried frown creased the space between Rhia's smooth brows.

Alice blinked and shook her head. Lovely. Not only was she obsessing over a near stranger, she was also hallucinating that she saw the same man, perfectly turned out in white tie and tails, chatting up her brother. "Did you see that tall blond man with Dami? They just went inside the tent."

"Dami? I didn't notice."

"You didn't notice Dami, or the man with him?"

"Either. Allie, really. Are you all right?"

"I'm beginning to wonder about that," she muttered.

"You're mumbling. Say again?"

Alice would have loved to drag her favorite sister off somewhere private, where she could tell her all about the scruffy, sexy, unforgettable stable hand—whom she could have sworn she'd just seen wearing a perfectly cut designer tailcoat and evening trousers and sharing a joke with their brother. She wanted a comforting hug and some solid, down-to-earth advice. But now was not the time. She tugged on Rhia's hand. "It doesn't matter. Come on. Let's go in. Marcus will be wondering where you've gone."

The family table was a long one, set up on a dais at the far end of the tent. All their brothers and sisters were there. The married ones had come with their spouses. Even dear Belle, who lived in America now with her horse-rancher husband, Preston McCade, had come all the way from Montana to celebrate with Rhia and Marcus. Only the little nieces and nephews were missing tonight. This was a grown-up party after all.

Rhia whispered, "We never have time to talk anymore."

"I know. I miss you, too."

"Come to our villa at seven Sunday night. We'll have dinner, catch up. Just the two of us."

"What about Marcus?"

"He's dining at the palace with Alex. Something about the CCU." Alexander, Damien's twin, was third-born of their brothers. Alex had created the elite fighting force the Covert Command Unit, in which Marcus served.

"I'll be there," Alice promised.

With a last hug, Rhia left her to join her groom in her seat of honor at the center of the table.

Alice went to greet her parents. Her mother, looking amazing as always in beaded black Chanel, gave her a kiss and a fond, "Hello, my darling," and didn't say a word about her tardiness. Her mother was like that. HSH Adrienne had high expectations, but she'd never been one to nag.

In the past, Alice had crashed a motorcycle in the marketplace, run off with a sheikh for a week in Marrakech, been photographed for *Vanity Fair* wearing only a cleverly draped silk scarf and been arrested in Beijing for participating in a protest march. Among other things.

Until Glasgow, her mother had never done more than gently remind her that she was a princess of Montedoro and expected to behave like one. But after Glasgow, for the first time, Alice had been summoned to her mother's office. HSH Adrienne had asked her to shut the door and then coolly informed her that she'd finally gone too far.

"Alice," her mother had said much too sadly, too gently, "it's one thing to be spirited and adventurous. It's another to be an embarrassment to yourself and our family. In future I am counting on you to exercise better judgment and to avoid situations that will lead to revealing, provocative pictures of you splashed across the front pages of the *Sun* and the *Daily Star*."

It had been awful. Just thinking about it made her feel a little sick to her stomach.

And sad, too. A bit wilted and grim.

Shake it off, she commanded herself. *Let it go.*

Alice looked for her place card and found it between her older sister Belle's husband, Preston McCade, and her younger sister Genevra. Genny wore shimmering teal-blue satin and was giggling over something with another sister, the youngest, Rory, who was seated on Genny's other side.

Damien sat at the opposite end of the table. No sign of the man who looked like Noah. Alice considered hustling down there and asking Dami...what?

Who was that man with the dark blond hair, the one you came in with?

And what if he stared at her blankly and demanded, *Allie, darling, what man?*

She waffled just long enough that she missed her

chance. Her mother rose and greeted the guests. A hush fell over the tent. Then her father stood, as well. He picked up his champagne glass to propose the first toast.

Allie reached for her glass, raised it high and drank on cue. Then she took her seat. She greeted her sisters and Preston, whom she liked a lot. He was charming and a little shy, with a great sense of humor. He bred and trained quarter horses, so they had plenty to talk about.

There were more toasts. Alice paced herself, taking very small sips of champagne, practicing being low-key and composed for all she was worth. By the time the appetizer was served, she felt glad she hadn't asked Dami about the broad-shouldered stranger with the dark gold hair and perfectly cut evening clothes.

It was nothing. It didn't matter. She would have a fine evening celebrating her dearest sister's hard-earned happiness. And no one else would know that she'd imagined she saw someone who wasn't really there. She accepted a second glass of champagne from a passing servant and picked up a spear of prosciutto-wrapped asparagus—and then almost dropped the hors d'oeuvre in her lap when she glanced over and saw Noah.

He wore the same perfect evening attire she'd glimpsed earlier. And he sat between a stunning blonde and a gorgeous redhead several tables away, staring right at her.

Chapter Two

Noah was watching Alice when she spotted him. Her mouth dropped open. Her face went dead white.

About then it occurred to him that maybe he'd carried his innocent deception a little too far.

She pressed her lips together and looked away, turning to her younger sister on her right side, forcing a smile. He waited for her to glance his way again.

Didn't happen.

Jennifer, the redhead seated on his left, put her hand on his thigh and asked him how he was enjoying his visit to Montedoro. He gently eased her hand away and said he was having a great time.

She hit him with a melting, eager look and said, "I'm so pleased to have met you, Noah, and I hope we can spend some time together during your stay. I would just love to show you the *real* Montedoro."

Andrea, the blonde on his other side, cut in, saving him the necessity of giving Jennifer an answer. "I love all of Prince Dami's friends," Andrea said. "Dami and I were once, well, very close. But then he met Vesuvia." A model and sometime actress, Vesuvia was often called simply V. "Dami is exclusive with V now," Andrea added. None of what she'd said was news to Noah. Or to anyone else, for that matter. "They're all over the tabloids, Dami and V," Andrea whispered breathlessly. She was mistress of the obvious in a big, big way.

"Or at least, the prince is *mostly* exclusive with V," Jennifer put in with a wicked little giggle. She fluttered her eyelashes at him. "I mean, they *are* always fighting and I notice that V's not here tonight...."

The meal wore on. Jennifer and Andrea kept up a steady stream of teasing chatter. Noah sipped champagne and hoped that Alice might grant him a second look.

If she did, he failed to catch it.

Had he blown it with her, misjudged her completely? It was starting to look that way.

But no. It couldn't be.

She'd assumed he was an itinerant stable hand and all he'd done was play along. He'd thought she would find the whole thing funny.

It hadn't even occurred to him that she might be upset about it. How could he have gotten it so wrong? He'd done his research on her after all. She was bold and curious and ready for anything, the darling of the scandal sheets. He'd never imagined she would freak out when she finally saw him as he really was.

So what did he do now?

He wouldn't give up, that was for damn sure. Not now that he'd met her, talked to her, seen her smile, looked in those eyes of hers that could be blue or gray or green, depending on the light and her shifting mood. Not now that he'd discovered she was *exactly* the woman he'd been looking for—and more.

Somehow he would have to make amends.

The meal finally ended. Princess Adrienne rose and congratulated the newlyweds again. She wished them a lifetime of married bliss. Then she invited the guests to enjoy the moonlit garden and to dance the night away in the palace ballroom upstairs.

Jennifer whispered an invitation in his ear. He turned to express his regrets.

When he glanced toward the dais again, Alice was gone.

Alice slipped out of the tent through the servants' entrance behind the dais.

She'd recovered from her initial shock at the sight of Noah sitting between those two beautiful women, looking as though he belonged there. At least by the end of dinner, she'd become reasonably certain she wasn't hallucinating. He was not a bizarre figment of her overactive imagination. The man who looked exactly like Noah the stable hand really did exist.

That meant she wasn't losing her mind after all—a fact she found wonderfully reassuring.

But *was* he actually the same man she'd first met sweeping the stable floor before dawn on Wednesday morning? Was this some kind of bizarre practical joke he was playing on her? And if so, did that make him a palace groom posing as a guest at the palace? Or a jetsetter friend of her brother's who enjoyed masquerading as the help?

She considered tracking down Dami and quizzing him about that friend of his who looked exactly like the poverty-stricken groom she'd met Wednesday.

But no. Not tonight. Damien might be able to enlighten her, but then he would have questions of his own. She just wasn't up for answering Dami's questions. And it didn't matter anyway. She knew what to do: forget it. Forget *him*.

It was all too weird. It made no sense and she wasn't going to think about it.

She would enjoy the rest of the evening and move on.

A familiar voice behind her said, "Allie, I haven't seen you in ages."

She turned to smile at a longtime friend. "Robert. How have you been?"

"I can't complain." Robert Bentafaille was compact and muscular, with an open face and kind green eyes. The Bentafailles owned orange groves. Lots of them. He and Alice were the same age and had gone through primary and secondary school together. "You look beautiful, as always."

"And you always say that."

"I hear the orchestra." He cast a glance back at the palace, at the lights blazing in the upstairs ballroom. Music drifted down to them. He offered his hand.

She took it and they turned together to go inside.

Alice danced two dances with Robert.

Then another longtime friend, Clark deRoncleff, tapped Robert on the shoulder. She turned into Clark's open arms and danced some more.

After that she left the floor, accepted a glass of sparkling water from a passing servant and visited with Rhia and Marcus for a bit. Rhia was sharing her plans for the nursery when Alice spotted Dami across the dance floor. He was talking to the man who almost certainly was Noah. She stared for a moment too long.

The man who had to be Noah seemed to sense her gaze on him. He turned. Their eyes met. His were every bit as blue as she remembered.

She had no doubt now. It had to be him. Quickly, she

turned away and gave her full attention to Rhia and her groom.

Noah didn't matter to her. She hardly knew him. She refused to care what he was doing there at her sister's wedding party or what he might be up to.

Marcus asked Rhia to dance. They went off together, holding hands, looking so happy it made Alice feel downright misty-eyed and more than a little bit envious.

Her eldest brother, Maximilian, came toward her. The heir to their mother's throne, Max was handsome and magnetic—like all of her brothers. He used to be a happy man. But three years ago his wife, Sophia, had died in a waterskiing accident. Max had loved Sophia since they were children. Now he was like a ghost of himself. He went through all the motions of living. But some essential element was missing. Sophia had given him two children, providing him with the customary heir and a spare to the throne. He didn't have to marry again—and he probably never would.

"We hardly see you lately," Max chided. "You haven't been to Sunday breakfast in weeks." It was a family tradition: Sunday breakfast in the sovereign's private apartments at the palace. She and her siblings were grown now, but they all tried to show up for the Sunday-morning meal whenever they were in Montedoro.

"I've been busy with my horses."

"Of course you have." Max leaned closer. "You did nothing wrong. Don't ever let them crush your spirit."

She knew whom he meant by *them:* the paparazzi and the tabloid journos. "Oh, Max…"

"You are confident and curious. You like to get out and mix it up. It's who you are. We all love you as you are and we know it was only in fun."

"I'm not so sure about Mother."

"She's on your side and she never judges. You know that."

"What I know is that I've finally managed to embarrass her." It wasn't so much that she'd French-kissed a girl. It was the pictures. They came off so tacky, like something out of *Girls Gone Wild*.

"I think you're wrong. Mother is not embarrassed. And she loves you unconditionally."

Alice didn't have the heart to argue about it, to insist that their mother *was* embarrassed; she'd said so. Instead, she leaned close to him and whispered, "Thank you."

He smiled his sad smile. "Dance?" Though Max would never marry again, women were constantly trying to snare him. They all wanted to console the widower prince who would someday rule Montedoro. So he tried to steer clear of them. At balls, he danced with his mother and his sisters and then retired early.

"I would love to dance with you." She pulled him out onto the floor and they danced through the rest of that number and the next one.

Before they parted, he asked her directly to come to the family breakfast that Sunday. "Please. Say you'll be here. We miss you."

She gave in and promised she would come, and then she walked with him to where their youngest sister, Rory, chatted with Lani Vasquez. Small, dark-haired and curvy, Lani was an American, an aspiring author of historical novels set in Montedoro. She'd come from America with Sydney O'Shea when Sydney had married Rule, the second-born of Alice's brothers.

Alice had assumed Max would dance next with Rory.

But he took Lani's hand instead. The music started up again and Max led the pretty American onto the floor.

Rory said, "Well, well."

"My, my," Alice murmured in agreement. For a moment the two sisters watched in amazement as their tragically widowed eldest brother danced with someone who wasn't his sister.

Then a girlfriend of Rory's appeared out of the crowd. She grabbed Rory's hand and towed her toward the open doors to the balcony. Alice considered following them. It was a lovely night. She could lean on the stone railing and gaze out over the harbor, admire the lights of the casino and the luxury shops and hotels that surrounded it.

"Alice. Dance with me."

The deep, thrilling voice came from directly behind her and affected her just as it had when they were alone in the stables. It seemed to slip beneath her skin, to shiver its way along the bumps of her spine, to create a warm pool of longing down in the deepest core of her.

She didn't turn. Instead, she stared blindly toward the open doors to the balcony. She wasn't even going to acknowledge him. She would start walking and she wouldn't look back.

If he dared to come after her, she would cut him dead.

But really, what would that prove? That she was afraid to deal with him? That she didn't have the stones to stand her ground and face him, to find out from his own mouth what kind of game he was playing with her? That Max had been right and the tacky tabloid reporters, the shameless paparazzi, really had done it? They'd broken her spirit, made her into someone unwilling to face a challenge head-on.

Oh, no. No way.

She whirled on him and glared into his too-blue eyes. "It *is* you."

He nodded. He held out his hand. "Let me explain. Give me that chance."

She kept her arm at her side. "I don't trust you."

"I know." He didn't lower his hand. The man had nerves of steel.

And she couldn't bear it, to let him stand there with his hand offered and untaken. She laid her fingers into his palm. Heat radiated up her arm just from that first contact. Her breath caught and tangled in her chest.

How absurd. Breathe.

With slow care, she sucked in a breath and then let it out as he turned and led her onto the floor. She went into his arms. They danced.

He had the good sense to hold her lightly. For a few endless minutes, neither of them spoke, which was just as well as far as Alice was concerned. She longed to wave her arms about and shriek accusations at him. Unfortunately, shrieking and waving her arms would attract attention, and that would no doubt land her on the front pages of the tabloids again.

She caught a hint of his aftershave. Evergreen and citrus, the same as before. It was all too disorienting. She'd thought he was one person and now here he was, someone else altogether. She felt shy. Tongue-tied. Young.

And at a definite disadvantage. She needed to take back the upper hand here. She had questions for him. And he'd better have good answers.

The next song began, a fast one. Couples separated and danced facing each other, moving to the beat but not touching. Noah didn't let her go, just picked up the rhythm a bit and danced them out of the way of the others.

"You're angry," he said at last.

"What happened to your two girlfriends?"

"What girlfriends?"

"That sexy redhead and the stunning blonde."

"They're not my girlfriends." He kept his voice low, but he did pull her fractionally closer. She allowed that in order to hear him over the music. "They were seated on either side of me at dinner, that's all."

"They seemed very friendly." She spoke quietly, too. She didn't want anyone overhearing, broadcasting their conversation, starting new rumors about her.

He held her even closer and whispered much too tenderly, "Is that somehow my fault?"

She fumed in silence, refusing to answer. Finally, she demanded, "Who are you, really?"

"I'm who I said I was."

"Noah."

"Yes."

"Do you have a last name?"

"Cordell." He turned her swiftly and gracefully to the music, guiding her effortlessly, keeping them to the outer edges of the floor.

"*Are* you a stable hand?"

"No. And I didn't say I was. You assumed that."

"And you never bothered to enlighten me. Do you live in Los Angeles?"

"No. Not for years. I have an estate in Carpinteria, not far from Santa Barbara. I live there most of the time. I also have a flat I keep in London. And a Paris apartment."

"So you should have no trouble affording that Akhal-Teke you said you want."

"No trouble at all. But it's a specific horse I'm after."

She should have known. "Let me guess. One of mine?"

"Orion."

She drew in a sharp breath. In that foolish dream of hers, he'd been riding Orion. "I'm not selling you Orion." That was a bit petty, and she knew it. Not to mention a bad business move. Alice bred her horses for sale—to buyers who would love them and bond with them and treat them well, buyers who appreciated the beauty and rarity of the breed. Her pool of buyers was a small one, as she also demanded a high price for her Tekes. She might be angry with Noah, but he knew horses and loved them. She'd be smarter not to reject him out of hand—as a potential buyer, anyway. "I don't wish to discuss my horses with you right now."

"You brought it up." The next song was a slower one. He effortlessly adjusted to the change in tempo, all the while gazing down at her, watching her mouth. As if he planned to kiss her—a bold move he had better not try.

She accused, "I brought it up as an example of the way that you lied to me. Not with words, maybe. But by implication. By action. The first time I saw you, you were sweeping the stable floor. Gilbert seemed to know you. What else was I to assume but that he'd hired you?"

"Gilbert was joking with me. He saw me sweeping and asked me if I needed a job. Your brother Damien had introduced us the day before. Dami knows I love horses and wanted me to have a chance to ride while I was here. And I had told him I was hoping to buy one of your stallions. He said I would have to talk to you about that."

"You're great friends, then, you and my brother?"

"Yes. I consider Damien a friend."

She thought again of the blonde and the redhead at

dinner. He'd seemed to take their fawning attentions as his due. "You're a player. Like Dami."

"I'm single. I enjoy a good life and I like the company of beautiful women."

"You're a player."

"I am not playing you, Alice." He held her gaze. Steadily. Somehow the very steadiness of his regard excited her.

She did not wish to be excited. "You've been playing me from the moment you picked up that broom and pretended to be someone you're not."

"Everything I told you was true. Everything. Yes, I've got all I'll ever need now, but I started out in L.A. with nothing. My parents were both dead by the time I was twenty-one. I have one sister, Lucy."

"And you went to work on a ranch when you were eighteen?"

"No. I visited that ranch. Often. My boss took a liking to me. He flipped houses in Los Angeles for a living and he hired me as a day laborer to start. I learned the business from the ground up, beginning on his low-end properties in East L.A."

"You're saying you learned fast?" She wasn't surprised.

"Before the crash, I was buying and selling in all the major markets. I got out ahead of the collapse with a nice nest egg. Now I manage my investments and I do what I want with the rest of my time. Oh, and that second cousin you mentioned, the one who lives in Bel Air?"

"Jonas."

He nodded. "I know him. Jonas Bravo and I have done business on a couple of occasions. He's a good man." He pulled her a little closer again. She allowed that, though she knew that she probably shouldn't. They danced without talking for a minute or two.

Finally, she muttered grudgingly, "You should have told me all of this at the first."

"I can see that now." He sounded so...sincere. As though he truly regretted misleading her.

She tried not to soften. "Why didn't you, then?"

"Alice, I..." The words trailed off.

"At a loss? I don't believe it. Just tell me. Why weren't you honest with me from the first?"

"I don't know, exactly. Because it was fun. Exciting. To tease you."

She started to smile and caught herself. "That's not a satisfactory answer."

"Look. I came early to ride and I saw you there, saddling that beautiful mare. It was still dark out and there was no one else around. I didn't want to scare you. I picked up the broom and started sweeping, because what's more nonthreatening than some guy sweeping the floor? And then... I don't know. You thought I was a groom and you talked to me anyway. I liked that. I got into it, that's all. In a way, the Noah you met in the stables really is me. Just...another possible me. The one who didn't make a fortune in real estate. I thought it would be something we would laugh over later."

The dance ended. For a moment they swayed together at the edge of the floor. She should have pulled away.

She stayed right where she was.

He was getting to her. She was liking him again. Believing the things he told her....

Yet another song started.

He pulled her even closer and whispered, his breath warm across her skin, "I screwed up, okay?" He whirled her around. They danced in a circle along the outer rim of the floor.

"You knew who I was from the first. Before we met. Right?"

He pulled back enough to give her a look. Patient. Ironic. "Please. I'm friends with your brother. He's told me about you—and your sisters and brothers. Also, I want one of your stallions and I know you're quite a horse trader, not only brutal when striking a bargain but particular about whom you'll sell to. I've made it my business to learn everything I can about you."

Which meant he would have seen the Glasgow pictures.

Well, so what? She'd done what she'd done. She'd gone over the top and she'd suffered for it. She was tired of being ashamed. "You know all about me? That sounds vaguely stalkerish."

He shrugged, his muscular shoulder lifting and then settling under her hand. "You could look at it that way, I suppose. Or you could admit that it's just good sense to find out what you can about the people you'll be dealing with."

"So of course you won't mind if I track you down online the next chance I get."

"I would expect nothing less." And he smiled, rueful. And somehow hopeful, too. He was way too charming when he smiled. "And when you find out I've told the truth, do I get another chance with you?"

All at once she was too sharply aware of his hand holding hers, his warm fingers and firm palm at her back, his big body brushing hers. Little arrows of sensation seemed to zip around beneath her skin. "A chance with me? I thought we were talking about your buying Orion."

He eased her closer. His breath touched her hair and his body burned into hers. Her skin felt electrified. And he whispered, "You know we're talking about more than the horse. Who's lying now? Ma'am?"

She liked it too much, dancing so close to him. She liked *him* too much. "Please don't hold me so tightly."

He instantly obeyed, loosening his hold so he embraced her easily, lightly, again. "Better?"

She nodded, thinking that this particular Noah, self-assured and sophisticated in evening dress, was every bit as brash and manly as the one she'd assumed was a groom. And smooth, too. She hadn't planned to forgive him for pretending to be a penniless stable hand—but somehow she already had.

And not only had she forgiven him, she was actually considering letting him have Orion after all. Because she did like him and she'd seen him with her horses. Orion would thrive in Noah's care.

He pulled her closer again. She allowed that. It felt good and she wasn't really afraid of him. She was afraid of *herself,* of her too-powerful response to him. And then there was her basic problem: it had always been so easy for her to get carried away. She would have to watch herself.

Then again, her goal tonight had been to get out and have a little fun.

So all right. It shouldn't be too difficult to do both— to have a little fun and yet not get carried away.

They danced the rest of that dance without talking. When it ended, they swayed together until the next dance began and then danced some more.

"Walk in the garden with me," he said when that song was over.

"Yes. I would like that."

He took her hand and led her from the dance floor.

It was going pretty well, Noah thought as he walked with her down the stone stairway that led to the big tent and the palace gardens beyond. She seemed to have gotten past her fury with him for pretending to be someone he wasn't. But he sensed a certain residual wariness in her. Which was fine. Few things worth winning came easily.

"Something to drink?" he asked.

"I would like that."

So they stopped in the tent, where waiters offered wine and cocktails and soft drinks, too. They both took flutes of champagne and went out the back exit behind the dais into the moonlit garden strung with party lights.

She said, "You implied when we talked in the stables that you were staying in Montedoro indefinitely.…"

"Not anymore. It turns out there are a couple of meetings I have to get back for. I'll be leaving Thursday."

"Is your sister visiting with you?"

"No, she's at home in California."

"I assume Dami has you staying here at the palace?"

He shook his head. "Lots of guests at the palace this weekend. I went ahead and took a suite at the Belle Époque." The five-star hotel was across from Casino d'Ambre.

Another couple came toward them. They nodded in greeting as they passed. When it was just the two of them again, Alice said, "I love the Belle Époque. We used to go for afternoon tea there now and then when I was a girl, my sisters and I. We would get our favorite table—on the mezzanine of the winter garden, with that amazing dome of stained glass and steel overhead. I would stuff myself with tea cakes, and the governess, Miss Severly, would have to reprimand me."

"Governess? I thought your brother said you all went to Montedoran schools."

"We did. But after we grew out of our nanny, Gerta, we also had Miss Severly. She tutored us between school terms and tried to drum good manners into us."

"Were you scared of your governess?"

"Not in the least. Once reprimanded, I only grew more determined. At tea I would wait until Miss Severly looked the other way and then try to stuff down as many cakes as I could before she glanced at me again."

"Did you make yourself sick?"

She slanted him a glance. "How did you know?"

He thought of all the tabloid stories he'd read about her. Of course she'd been a girl who gobbled cakes when the governess wasn't looking. "Just a guess."

They came out on a point overlooking the sea. An iron bench waited beneath a twisted cypress tree and an iron railing marked the cliff's edge. Alice went to the railing. She sipped her champagne and stared out over the water at the distant three-quarter moon.

As he watched her, he had the oddest feeling of unreality. It was like a dream, really, being there with her. She was a vision in lustrous red, her bare shoulders so smooth, her arms beautifully shaped, muscular in a way that was uniquely feminine.

Eventually, she turned to him. Her eyes were very dark at that moment. Full of shadows and secrets. "I've never been as well behaved as I should be. It's a problem for me. I'm too eager for excitement and adventure. But I'm working on that."

He moved to stand beside her, and leaned back against the railing. "There's nothing wrong with a little adventure now and then."

She laughed, turning toward him, holding her champagne glass up so he could tap his against it. "I agree. But as you said, *now and then.* For me it's like the tea cakes. I just *have* to eat them all." She sighed. And then she drained the glass. "So I'm trying to slow down a little, to think before I jump, to be less…excitable."

"It's a shame to curb all that natural enthusiasm." He wanted to touch her—to smooth her shining hair or run the back of a finger along the sleek curve of her neck. But he held himself in check. He didn't want to spook her.

"Everybody has to grow up sometime." She leaned in closer. Her perfume came to him: like lilies and leather and a hint of the ocean. He could stand there and smell her all night. But she was on the move again. In a rustle of red skirts, she went to the bench and sat down. "Tell me about your sister." She bent to set her empty glass beneath the bench.

"She's much younger than I am. We're twelve years apart. She's been homeschooled for most of her life. She's sensitive and artistic. She could always draw, from when she was very little, and she carries a sketch pad around with her all the time. And she loves to sew. She's better with a thread and needle than any tailor I've ever used. She makes all her own clothes. And now she's suddenly decided that she wants to study fashion design in New York City."

Alice patted the space next to her. "And you don't want her to do what she wants?"

He went to her. She swept her skirt out of the way and he sat beside her. "Lucy was homeschooled because she was sick a lot. She almost died more than once. She had asthma and a problem with a heart valve."

"Had?" She took his empty champagne flute and put it under the bench with hers. "You mean she's better now?"

"The asthma's in remission. And after several surgeries that didn't do much good, two years ago she finally had the one that actually worked."

"So she's well? She can lead a normal life."

"She has to be careful."

Alice was studying him again, and much too closely. "You're overprotective."

"I'm not." He sounded defensive and he knew it.

"But Lucy thinks so…."

He grumbled, "You're too damn smart." He could almost regret not choosing a stupid princess. But then all he had to do was look at her, smell her perfume, hear her laugh, watch her with her horses—and he knew that no silly, malleable princess would do for him. Alice was the one. No doubt about it.

"I certainly am smart," she said. "So you'd better be honest with me from now on. Tell me lies and I'll find you out."

"I *have* been honest." Mostly.

She shook her head. "Do I have to remind you of your alter ego, the stable hand—again?"

"Please. No." He held up both hands palms out in surrender.

"Oh, my." She pretended to fan herself. "You're begging. I think I like that."

He set her straight. "It was a simple request."

"No, no, no." She laughed. She had a great laugh, full-out and all in. "You were definitely begging." Smiling smugly, showing off the dimples that made her almost as cute as she was beautiful, she asked, "You said Lucy is twenty-three, right?"

He kept catching himself watching her mouth. It was plump and pretty and very tempting. But he wasn't going to kiss her, not tonight. He'd just barely salvaged the situation with her and he couldn't afford to push his luck by moving too fast. "Why are we talking about Lucy, anyway?"

"Because she's important to you." She said it simply. Openly.

And all at once he wanted to be…better somehow. It was bewildering. She stirred him, more than he'd ever intended to be stirred. He started talking, started saying *real* things. "When our mom died, we had nothing. Lucy was nine and sick all the time. I was twenty-one, just starting out, working days for that guy with the horse ranch I told you about, taking business classes at night. Our mom died and Child Protective Services showed up the next day to take Lucy away."

"I am sorry…." She said it softly, the three simple words laden with sadness. For him.

He wanted some big things from her. Sympathy wasn't one of them. "Don't be. It was a good thing."

"A good thing that you lost your sister?"

"I didn't lose her. She went to an excellent foster mom, a great lady named Hannah Russo who made me welcome whenever I came to visit."

"Well, that's good."

"It was, yeah. And that they wouldn't let me take care of my sister was a definite wake-up call. I knew I had to get my ass in gear or I would never get custody of her. She was so damn frail. She could have died. I was afraid she *would* die. It was seriously motivating. I was determined, above all, to get her back with me where I could take care of her."

Her eyes were so soft. He could see the moon in them. "How long did it take you?"

"I got custody of her three years after our mom died, when Lucy was twelve. I've taken care of her since then. She's my family. Sometimes she doesn't see it, but I only want what's best for her."

"I know you do." She leaned in close again. He smelled lilies and sea foam. "I like you, Noah." She said his name on a breath. And then she leaned closer still. "You're macho and tough. Kind of. But not. You confuse me. I shouldn't like that. But I do. I like *you* far too much, I think."

He whispered, "Good." His senses spun. She affected him so strongly. Too strongly, really. More strongly than any woman had in a long, long time—maybe ever. Above all, he had to remember not to push too fast. Not to kiss her. Yet.

Her red skirts rustled as she leaned that little bit closer. Her breath brushed his cheek, so warm, so sweet.

What now? Should he back off? Did it count as moving too fast if *she* was the one doing the moving?

She whispered, "I promised myself I wouldn't kiss you...."

"All right." It wasn't all right. Not really. And she was too close, making it way too hard to remember that he wasn't going to kiss her. Not now. Not tonight....

"But, Noah. I really *want* to kiss you."

He held very still, every molecule in his body alert. Hungry. He wanted to go for it, to grab her and haul her into his aching arms. He wanted that way too much for his own peace of mind. "Remember," he said on a bare husk of sound, "you have a plan."

"What plan?" Her gaze kept straying to his mouth.

"You promised yourself you would think before you jump." Did he mean to be helpful? Maybe. But somehow it came out as a challenge.

And, as everything he'd read about her had made crystal clear, Her Highness Alice never could resist a challenge. "To hell with my plan."

"Tomorrow you'll feel differently."

"Tomorrow can take care of itself." She swayed that fraction closer. "Right now I only want to kiss you." She lifted those plump, sweet lips to him.

He made himself wait. He managed, just barely, to hold himself in check until her mouth touched his.

Then, with a low groan, he reached out and wrapped his arms good and tight around her.

Chapter Three

Alice knew very well that she shouldn't be kissing him.

Kissing him, after all, was exactly what she'd said she wouldn't do.

But the scent of him was all around her—like his big strong arms that held her so very tightly. His chest was broad and hard and wonderful beneath the snow-white evening shirt.

And his kiss? Deep and demanding at first, thrilling her. His hot breath burned her mouth; his tongue delved in.

But then a moment later he dialed it down, going gentle, easier. He tempted her all the more forcefully by using tenderness, by taking it slow. His big hands roamed her back, making her shiver with delight. And his lips... Oh, my, the man certainly did know how to kiss. She could go on like this forever, sitting under the moon with the soft sigh of the sea far below them, all wrapped up in Noah's arms.

Then again, anyone might come up on them out here in the open like this. The paparazzi were everywhere. She'd learned that the hard way, over and over again.

If someone got a shot of her now, plastered all over a virtual stranger, soul-kissing him deeper than she had that redheaded barmaid during the karaoke escapade...

With a low moan, she put her hands to his hard chest and pushed him away. He made no move to stop her.

Breathless, still yearning, she faced forward again. Sagging against the iron back of the bench, she stared out beyond the railing at the moonlit sea.

Noah said nothing. She was grateful for that.

Back on the path behind them, a woman laughed. It was more of a giggle, really. A man spoke as though in reply, his voice low and intimate, the words unclear. More feminine laughter, and then the man said something else, the sound of his voice retreating as he spoke. Whoever they were, they had turned and gone back toward the palace.

There was silence. Only the breeze off the sea and the distant cry of a gull.

Alice smoothed her hair and straightened the bodice of her strapless gown. "Sometimes I really disappoint myself."

"Is it possible you're trying too hard to be good?" he asked in that lovely sexy rumble that had stirred her from the first.

She shot him a scoffing glance. "More likely, I'm not trying hard enough."

He caught her hand. Before she could pull away, he pressed his wonderful lips to the back of it. His mouth was so warm, so deliciously soft compared to the rest of him. "You're amazing. Just as you are. Why mess with a great thing?" His words were pure temptation. She wanted only to sigh and sway against him again, to kiss him some more, to give him a chance to flatter her endlessly. She wanted to let him kiss her and touch her until she forgot all the promises she'd made to herself about learning a little discipline, about keeping her actions under control.

Instead, she said, "I would like my hand back, please." He released her. She rose and brushed out her taffeta skirt. "Good night. Please don't follow me." She turned for the trail, glancing back only once before she ducked between the hedges.

He hadn't moved. He sat facing the sea, staring out at the moon.

Alice collected her bag and wrap from the attendant at the side entrance and called for her driver.

Twenty minutes after she'd left Noah staring out to sea, the driver was holding the limo door for her. She slipped into the plush embrace of the black leather seat.

At home she had another bath. A long one, to relax.

But she didn't relax. She lay there amid the lily-scented bubbles and tried not to feel like a complete jerk.

Noah had really stepped up. He'd made an honest, forthright apology for misleading her at the stables. And then he'd gone about being a perfect gentleman. He'd also been open and honest with her about his life, his past. About the tensions between him and his little sister.

He had not put a move on her. She'd made sure that he wouldn't, by going on and on about how from now on she planned to look before she leaped.

After which she had grabbed him and kissed him for all she was worth.

Seriously, now. She was hopeless. She needed a keeper, someone to follow her around and make sure she behaved herself. Twenty-five years old and she couldn't stop acting like an impulsive, greedy child.

Her bath grew cold. She only grew more tense, more annoyed with herself.

Finally, she got out and dried off and put on a robe. It was after two in the morning. Time for bed.

But she couldn't sleep. She kept thinking how Noah had said he had no problem with her looking him up on the internet.

Finally, she threw back the covers, grabbed her laptop and snooped around for a while.

She learned that everything he'd told her that night— and in the stables, for that matter—was the truth. He was quite a guy, really, to have come from a run-down rented bungalow in the roughest part of Los Angeles without a penny to his name and built a real-estate empire before he was thirty. When he was twenty-eight, he'd been one of *Forbes'* thirty top entrepreneurs under thirty. Two years ago he'd been a *People* magazine pick for one of America's ten most eligible bachelors. His Santa Barbara–area estate had been profiled in *House & Garden*.

There were several pages of images. Some of them showed him with Lucy, who had a sweet, friendly smile and looked very young. But most of them were of him with a gorgeous woman at his side—a lot of *different* gorgeous women. He'd never been linked to any one woman for any length of time.

The endless series of beautiful girlfriends reminded her of all the reasons she wouldn't be getting involved with him. The last thing she needed was to fall for a rich player who would trade her in for a newer model at the first opportunity.

It was after four when she finally fell asleep. She woke at noon, ate a quick breakfast, put on her riding clothes and went to the stables.

Noah wasn't there. Excellent. With a little luck, she would get through the last five days of his Montedoran visit without running into him again.

Sunday morning, Alice kept her promise to Max and went to breakfast at the palace. Everyone seemed happy to see her.

Her mother made a special effort to ask her how the plans were coming along for next year's Grand Champions Tour. Alice gave her a quick report and her mother said how pleased they all were with her work. She'd sold two mares, a stallion and a gelding in the past month. The money helped support her breeding program, but a good chunk of it went to important causes. Her mother praised her contribution to the lives of all Montedorans.

Alice basked in the approval. She knew what it meant. Her mother was getting past her disappointment over her antics in Glasgow.

At the table, she ended up next to Damien. He threw an arm across her shoulders and pressed a kiss to her cheek. "Allie. You're looking splendid, as always."

"Flatterer."

Dami shrugged and got to work on his eggs Benedict. He looked a little tired, she thought. But then, he often did. He was quite the globe-trotter. Most people thought he was all about beautiful women and the good life—and he was. But he also held a degree in mechanical engineering and design. He was a talented artist, too. And beyond all that, he loved putting together a profitable business deal almost as much as their second-born brother, Rule. And then there were the charities he worked hard to support.

No wonder he looked as though he needed a long nap.

She was tempted to ply him with questions about Noah. But what was the point? She'd already decided that she and Noah weren't going to be happening, so it didn't matter what Dami might have to tell her about him.

Dami sipped espresso. When he set down the demitasse, he turned to her again and said softly, "I heard you danced more than one dance with Noah Cordell last Friday. After which you went walking in the garden with him...."

Well, all right, then. Apparently, she was going to hear about Noah after all, whether she wanted to or not. "I met him in the stables. He was there Wednesday and Thursday mornings, early. He said you had introduced him to Gilbert."

"That's right."

"We...chatted."

"And danced," he repeated, annoyingly patient. "And walked in the garden."

"Yes, Dami. We did."

"You like him." It wasn't a question. His expression was unreadable.

She answered truthfully. "I do. He's intelligent, fun and a good dancer, as well."

"He's worse with women than I am."

"But you're not so bad—lately. I mean, what about Vesuvia?"

"What about her?" He gave her one of those looks. "We've been on-again, off-again. Now we're permanently off."

"I'm sorry to hear that."

"Don't be. It's for the best."

"But you've settled down a lot. We've all noticed."

He dismissed her argument with a wave. "I'm not a

good bet when it comes to relationships. Neither is Noah. It's always a new woman with him. Take my advice. Stay away from him."

That got her back up. "You ought to know better than to tell me what to do, Dami."

"It's for your own good, I promise you."

She laughed. "You're just making it worse. And you know that. You know how I am. Tell me *not* to do a thing and I just *have* to do it. Or are you *trying* to get me interested in Noah?"

"I'm not that clever."

"Oh, please. We both know you're brilliant."

"Sometimes, my darling, I actually do mean exactly what I say. Please stay away from Noah Cordell."

She really wanted to remind him that he had no right to tell her whom she could or couldn't see. But she let it go. "He wants to buy Orion."

"Do you want to sell him Orion?"

"I told him I wouldn't, but actually, I'm still thinking it over."

"I'll be honest."

"Why, thank you."

"I've been to his California estate. It's a horse farm and a fine one. And he's as good with horses as you are."

Alice had seen how good Noah was with horses. Still, her pride couldn't let that stand. "No one's as good with horses as I am."

"Plus, you're so enchantingly shy and modest."

"Shyness and modesty are overrated."

He turned back to his meal. They ate in silence for a minute or two. Then he said, "Noah's got more money than we do. He would pay whatever price you set for one of your Tekes. And he treats his animals handsomely."

"Then you do think I should sell him the stallion?"

"Yes—but then, I know you, Allie. You're going to do exactly what you want to do."

"I certainly am."

"Just don't let him charm you. Keep your guard up, or you'll get hurt."

Keep your guard up, or you'll get hurt....

Dami had only warned her of what she already knew. And she *would* heed his warning. For once, she wouldn't be contrary for contrary's sake. She would take her brother's advice and steer clear of Noah Cordell. Should she happen to meet up with him again, she would treat him with courtesy.

Courtesy and nothing more.

Her resolve got its first test at the stables that afternoon. Noah appeared as she was consulting with the equine dentist who checked the teeth of all her horses twice yearly. She glanced up and there he was out in the courtyard, the September sun gilding his hair, looking way too tall and fit and yummy for her peace of mind. Just the sight of him caused a curl of heat down low in her abdomen.

But no problem. She could handle this.

Alice asked the dentist to excuse her for a moment.

When Noah entered the stable, she was waiting for him, her smile cool and composed. "Noah. I hardly recognized you."

Gone were the old jeans and battered Western boots. Today he was beautifully turned out in the English style: black breeches, black polo shirt and a fine pair of black field boots. He regarded her distantly. "I was hoping to ride." A flick of a glance at the rows of stalls. "How about

Gadim?" The six-year-old black gelding had energy to spare and could be fractious.

But she knew Noah could handle him. "Excellent choice. Shall I call a groom to tack him up?"

"I can manage, thanks." His tone gave her nothing. Because she'd come on so distant and cool? Or because he'd already lost interest in her?

She couldn't tell.

And she wished that she didn't care.

"Good, then," she said too brightly. "Have a pleasant ride."

She returned to her consultation with the dentist, who had a list of the horses needing teeth pulled or filed.

Noah was off on Gadim when she finished with the dentist. She considered lingering until he came back. She wanted to ask him how he'd enjoyed his ride, to let him know that she might be convinced to sell him Orion.

But that would only be courting trouble.

She liked him too much. She could let down her guard with him so very easily. Not that he even cared at this point. He'd seemed so bored and uninterested earlier.

Which shouldn't matter in the least to her.

But it did.

No. Not a good idea to hang around in the hope of seeing him again.

She left the stables for a far paddock, where she spent the remainder of the afternoon working on leading and tying with a couple of recently weaned foals.

"Don't listen to Dami," Rhia said that evening as they shared dessert on the terrace of her villa overlooking the harbor.

Alice had told her sister everything by then. "But what if Dami's right?"

"That the man's a player? Oh, please. As though Dami has any room to talk."

"Well, but I just don't need to get myself into any more trouble. I really don't."

Rhia enjoyed a slow bite of her chocolate soufflé. "How are you going to get into trouble? You said he's filthy rich."

"Whether or not I get myself in trouble has nothing to do with how much money a man has."

"I *mean* you can rest assured that he's no fortune hunter. You're both single. You both love horses. You enjoy being with him. And you happen to be extremely attracted to him. You should give him a chance." She savored yet another bite. "Mmm." She licked chocolate from her upper lip. "Lately, if it's chocolate, I can't get enough."

"The baby must love chocolate," Alice suggested with a smile.

"That must be it—and what was it you once advised me? 'Rhia, be bold,' you said."

"Oh, please. That was about Marcus."

"So?"

"Marcus loves you. He's *always* loved you."

Rhia frowned. "I wasn't at all sure about that at the time."

"Still, my situation is entirely different."

"Why?"

"Because *we're* so different, you and I. You've always been nothing short of exemplary. Well behaved and *good*. You needed to be told to get out there and go after the only man you've ever loved. I don't require any such encouragement."

"On the contrary, it seems very clear to me that you do."

"One, Noah Cordell is not my lifelong love. I truly hardly know the man. And two, if anything, *I* need to be told *not* to be bold."

Her sister reached across the table and touched her cheek. "You like him. He likes you. You haven't been this worked up over a man in forever."

"I am not worked up."

Rhia clucked her tongue and then began scraping the last of the soufflé out of her ramekin. "I don't know what I'm going to do with you."

"Support me. Sympathize with me."

"As though that's going to help you." Rhia shook her head and licked her spoon.

"Even if I took your advice instead of Dami's, I'm afraid it's too late."

"Too late for what?"

"I'm afraid he's not interested in me anymore. Today in the stables, he acted as though he didn't even *care* what I thought of him."

"Was this before or after you treated him like a stranger?"

"I didn't treat him like a stranger."

"Yes, you did. You *said* that you did."

"I was perfectly civil."

"Civil. Precisely. Are you going to eat your soufflé?" Alice pushed it across the table.

Rhia dug right in, sighing. "Oh, my, yes. *So* good. And you do see what's happening here, don't you?"

"What?"

"You are not being you." Rhia paused to sigh over another big bite of chocolate. "And you're making yourself miserable."

"Not being me? Of course I'm being me. Who else would I be?"

"Allow me to explain…."

"Please."

Rhia pointed with her spoon. "You went a little over the top in Glasgow."

"A *little?*"

"That is what I said. You went over the top, and since then, you've decided you need to be *so* well behaved and subdued. It's just not like you at all. You are a brave, bold person, a person who jumps right into anything that interests her, who lives by her instincts. But you're trying to be someone else, someone careful and controlled, someone who plans ahead, who reasons everything out with agonizing care. And as your favorite sister who loves you more than you'll ever know, it's my responsibility to inform you that being someone you're not isn't working for you."

Alice thought a lot about the things Rhia had said to her. She could see the sense in Rhia's advice, she truly could.

But the thing was that she liked Noah *too* much. She hardly knew him, yet she couldn't stop thinking about him.

It scared her. It really did. She'd never been so powerfully attracted to any man before. What if she did fall in love with him?

And then he dumped her for someone else?

Even a brave, bold woman who lived by her instincts should have the sense not to volunteer for that kind of pain.

She didn't see him on Monday. But then Tuesday she went down to the Triangle d'Or, the area of exclusive shops near the casino, to pick up a Balenciaga handbag she'd ordered. She saw him sitting at a little outdoor café sipping an espresso. He was alone and she was so very tempted to stop and chat with him a little.

But she didn't. Uh-uh. She walked on by, quickly, before he could spot her and wave at her. Or worse, ignore her.

He was leaving on Thursday, he'd said. She only had to get through the next day without doing anything stupid. He would go home to his estate in California, to his frail and artistic little sister. And in time she would forget him.

All day Wednesday she kept thinking that tomorrow he would be gone. He never came to the stables that day—or if he did, she missed seeing him. She went home at a little after six.

Tomorrow he'll be gone....

She wanted to cry.

It was too much. She couldn't stand it anymore, that he would return to America and she might never see him again.

She did the very thing she knew she shouldn't do. She picked up the phone and called the Belle Époque. She asked for his room and they put her right through.

He answered the phone on the second ring. "Yes?"

"It's Alice. Are you still leaving tomorrow?" Her voice came out husky and confident. She sounded like the bold woman Rhia insisted she actually was.

"Alice. I'm surprised." *He* sounded anything but bored. But he didn't sound exactly happy, either.

"You're angry with me."

"Come on. I got the message when you ran away Friday night—and the other day in the stables when I came to ride. I got it loud and clear."

Her heart sank. "I'm sorry. I... Maybe I shouldn't have called."

A silence. And then, with real feeling, "Don't say that. I'm glad that you called."

"You are?"

"Yeah."

She let out a sigh of pure relief. "So, then, are you leaving?"

"Yes. Tomorrow."

"And tonight?" Her throat clutched. She coughed to clear it. "Are you busy tonight?"

Another silence. For a moment she thought he'd hung up. But then he asked, "What game are you playing now, Alice?"

"It's not a game. I promise you."

"Frankly, it feels like a game, a game I'll never win."

She tried for lightness. "Look at it this way—at least I'm not boring and predictable."

More dead air. And then at last he said, "I'm available. For you."

Well, all right. He definitely sounded like a man who wanted to see her again. Suddenly, she was floating on air. "I want to wear a long dress and diamonds. I want to play baccarat and eat at La Chanson." La Chanson de la Mer was right on the water in the Triangle d'Or and arguably the best restaurant on the Riviera.

"I'll arrange everything. Whatever you want."

Her stomach had gone all fluttery. Her heart was racing. Her cheeks felt too warm. Sweet Lord, she was out of control.

And it was fabulous. "Be in front of the casino, by the fountain," she commanded. "Eight o'clock."

"I'll be there."

Noah was waiting right where she'd told him to be, dressed for evening, feeling way too damned anxious to see her again, when her limo pulled up a few feet away.

The driver got out, hustled around and opened her door. She emerged in a strapless gold dress that clung to every sweet curve and had a slit up the skirt to above the knee. Her hair was pinned up loosely, bits of it escaping to curl at her nape.

And she was on her own, as he'd hoped. No bodyguard. Damien had told him that the princely family only used bodyguards outside the principality. Good. He might actually get a chance to be alone with her.

She saw him. A gorgeous, hopeful, glowing smile curved her lips. They stood there like a couple of lovesick teenagers, just looking at each other, as the driver got back behind the wheel and the long black car slid away.

They both started moving at the same time. Three steps and he was with her, in front of her, looking down into those amazing blue-green eyes.

Again, they just stared at each other. He said, "God. You're so beautiful."

And she said, "You came. I was a little worried you wouldn't."

"Are you kidding? Turn down a chance to spend an evening with you? Couldn't do it." Over her shoulder, he saw a man with a camera. "Someone's taking our picture."

"Behave with dignity," she said. "And ignore them. I'll do my very best to follow your lead. Because, as we both know, dignity was never my strong suit."

"You are more than dignified enough," he argued.

She gave him her full-out, beautiful laugh. "Not true, but thanks for trying."

He wanted to kiss her, but not while some idiot was snapping pictures of them. "Dinner first?"

"Perfect." She reached for his arm.

They turned for the restaurant. It was just a short walk across the plaza.

He'd gotten them a table on the patio, which jutted out over the water. The food was excellent and the waitstaff were always there when you needed them, but otherwise invisible. The sky slowly darkened and the moon over the water glowed brighter as the night came on. The sea glittered, reflecting the lights of the Triangle d'Or and those shining from the windows and gardens of the red-roofed villas that crowded the nearby hillsides.

They talked of nothing important during the meal, which was fine with him. He was content right then just to be with her, to listen to her laughter and watch those sweet dimples appear in her cheeks when she smiled.

After they ate, they strolled back across the plaza to the casino. They played craps and roulette and baccarat. People stopped to watch them, to whisper about them. A few took pictures. Noah had foreseen this and called ahead to speak with the manager so that the casino staff was on top of the situation. They made sure none of the gawkers got too close.

Alice won steadily and so did he. Around eleven he

challenged her to play blackjack, two-handed, in one of the exclusive back rooms.

She looked at him with suspicion. But in the end, as he could have predicted, she refused to walk away from a challenge. "Am I going to regret this?"

He simply offered his arm. When she wrapped her hand around it, he led her into the card room in the back, where the table he'd reserved was waiting for them, cordoned off with golden ropes in its own quiet little corner. She eyed the deck of cards and the equally divided stacks of chips as he pulled back her chair for her.

"I thought we would play for something more interesting than money." He pushed in her chair and went around to sit opposite her.

She cast a glance around the big room. Almost every other table was in use. Leaning closer, lowering her voice so only he heard her, she said, "I am not taking off my clothes in a room full of strangers."

He laughed. "Clearly, I should have ordered a private room."

She tried to play it stern but didn't quite succeed. Her dimples gave her away. "Let's just not go there."

"Fair enough." He shuffled the cards.

She watched him, narrow eyed. "All right, then. If not for money, then what?"

He looked up into her eyes. "Orion."

She stared at him for a count of three before she spoke. "Surely you're joking."

He shook his head. "If I win, you agree to sell him to me."

She looked at him sideways, her diamond earrings glittering, scattering the light from the chandeliers above.

"At my price, then. You're only winning the right to buy him."

"That's right."

"Think twice, Noah. It's an astronomical price."

"Name it."

She did.

He looked at her patiently—and counteroffered.

She laughed, glanced away—and then countered his counter.

"Agreed." He slapped the deck in front of her.

Alice cut the cards. "But what if *I* win?"

He took the deck again. "Name your prize."

"Hmm." She grinned slowly. "I know. I want you to donate twenty thousand American dollars to St. Stephens Children's Home. My brother-in-law Marcus was raised there."

He gave her a wry smile. "So either way, I pay."

She dimpled. "Exactly."

He pretended to think it over. Then, "At least it's a worthy cause. Done."

They began to play.

She was an excellent gambler, bold and focused. And fearless, as well. She kept track of the cards seemingly without effort, laughing and chatting so charmingly as she played.

He was down to a very short stack at one point. But he battled his way back, winning. Losing. And then winning again.

It was almost two in the morning when he claimed her last chip from her.

She leaned back in her chair and laughed. "All right, Noah. You win. You may buy Orion for the price we agreed on."

He got the real picture then. "You were going to sell him to me anyway."

Her smile was downright smug. "Yes, I was—and enough of all this." She held out both hands, as though to indicate the whole of the world-famous casino complex. "Let's go somewhere else."

An attendant showed them to a private office where Noah settled up and they collected what they'd won earlier in the evening. The attendant appeared again with Alice's gold wrap and tiny jeweled handbag. A few minutes later they emerged into the glittering Montedoran night.

"What now?" he asked, even though it was a risk; it gave her an out if she suddenly decided she should call it a night. He was betting she wouldn't. She seemed to be having a great time. And he already knew how much she enjoyed calling the shots.

"Somewhere private." She glanced across the plaza where two men with cameras were snapping away. "Somewhere we can talk and not be disturbed."

Noah chuckled, pleased with himself that he'd read her mood correctly. "As though there's anywhere in Montedoro they won't follow us."

She took hold of his arm again and leaned close. He breathed in her scent. Exciting. So sweet. She said, "I have a plan."

"Uh-oh."

She laughed. "That's exactly what my sister Rhia always says when I come up with a fabulous idea." She faked a puzzled frown. "Why is that, do you think?"

He played it safe. "Not a clue."

"Ha!" And then she leaned even closer. "I am having altogether too much fun."

Her words pleased him no end. "There's no such thing as too much fun."

"Yes, there is. But it's all right. It's your last night in Montedoro after all. And we may never see each other again."

Wrong. "I just bought a horse from you, remember?"

"Of course I remember. And you shall have Orion. But you know what I meant."

He decided to let that remark go, but if she thought this was the last evening they would spend together, she didn't know who she was dealing with. "Tell me your plan."

"You're sure? A moment ago you seemed reluctant to hear it."

"I'm sure."

"Well, all right, then." She whispered her scheme in his ear.

Chapter Four

"It just might work," he said, admiring the way the bright lights brought out hints of auburn and gold in her hair.

"Of course it will work."

"All right, then. I'm game." They turned together for his hotel, neither looking back to see if they were being followed. Why bother to look? Of course they were being followed. The paparazzi were relentless. As they entered the lobby, he got out his cell and called his driver.

He led her straight through to the elevators. They got on and rode up to his floor—after which they changed elevators and went back down to the mezzanine level.

They took the service stairway to the first floor again and slipped out the side door, where the car he'd called for was waiting, the engine running. The driver, Talbot, held the door for her. Noah jumped in on the other side.

"Where to?" Talbot asked once they were safely hidden from prying eyes behind tinted windows. Alice rattled off a quick series of directions. The driver nodded and pulled the car away from the curb.

Noah raised the panel between the front and rear seats.

Alice glanced at him and grinned. "Alone at last."

He wrapped his arm around her and drew her closer. "If I kiss you, will you run away again?"

She gazed at him steadily, eyes shining. Then she shook her head. "Not while the car is moving."

He bent closer and brushed his lips across the velvet flesh of her temple. "Remind me to tell Talbot never to stop...."

"It's a tempting idea, being here with you forever...." She tipped her face up to him.

He brushed his mouth across hers, giving her a moment to accept him. When her lips parted slightly on a small tender sigh, he deepened the contact.

She let him in. He tasted the wet, secret surfaces behind her lips, ran his tongue along the smooth, even edges of her pretty white teeth.

Another sigh from her, deeper than the one before.

And he tightened his arm around her, bringing her closer so he could taste her more deeply still.

When she brought her hand up between them and pushed lightly against his chest, he lifted his mouth from hers just enough to grumble, "What now, Alice?"

Her eyes had the night in them. "Dami told me to stay away from you. He says you're a heartbreaker." Bad words scrolled through his mind, but he held them in. She added, "My sister Rhia told me not to listen to Dami."

"I like your sister already." He kissed her again, quickly, a little more ruthlessly than he probably should have. "And I'll talk to your brother."

Her fingers strayed upward. She stroked the nape of his neck. He wished she'd go on doing that for a century or two. "Please don't talk to Dami about me. It's none of his business. He doesn't get to decide who I see or don't see."

Noah had pretty much expected Damien to warn Alice off him. He'd considered explaining his real goal to Dami up front when he'd told Dami he wanted Orion—but he'd decided against it.

Damien wouldn't have believed him anyway. And Alice might be convinced to let him off the hook for a lot of things. But even before their first meeting, he'd known enough about her to figure out that she would never forgive him for telling her brother his real intentions before he revealed them to her.

And come on. He'd never planned to tell her *or* her brother everything. He'd assumed the whole truth wouldn't fly with either of them. The idea had been to meet her, pursue her and win her. To sweep her off her pretty feet.

But now that he'd come to know her a little, he was having second thoughts about the original plan. She was honest. Forthright. And after the near disaster of his playing along when she mistook him for a stable hand, he'd learned his lesson: she expected him to be honest, too.

Which brought him to that other thing, the thing he hadn't been prepared for. The way she made him want to give her everything, to be more than he'd ever been.

It was getting beyond his pride now, way past his idea of who he was and what he'd earned in his life. It was getting downright personal.

She *mattered* to him now, as a person. He didn't really understand it or want to think on it too deeply. It was what it was.

And it meant that he would knock himself out to give her whatever she needed, whatever she wanted from him. Up to and including the unvarnished truth.

So, then. He hadn't decided yet. Should he go there— go all the way, lay the naked truth right out on the table for her?

It was dangerous, a bold move.

Too bold?

Could be. And probably not tonight, anyway. It seemed much too soon....

She laid her soft hand against the side of his face. "Earth to Noah. Are you in there?"

"Forget about Damien." He said it too fiercely, and he knew it. "Kiss me again."

She laughed—and then she kissed him. And then she settled against him with her head on his shoulder and asked, "How did you meet my brother?"

He breathed in the scent of her hair. "I thought we were going to forget about Damien."

She tipped her head up and grinned at him. "You wish—and seriously. How did you meet him?"

"At a party in New York a little over two years ago. We both knew the host. I struck up a conversation with him. We found we had a lot in common."

"Fast cars, beautiful women..."

He shrugged. "I like your brother. We get along—as a rule, anyway."

The car pulled to a stop.

"We're here." She straightened from his embrace. With reluctance, he let her go and lowered the panel between the seats.

"Will you be getting out, sir?" Talbot asked.

"Yes, thanks." The driver jumped out to open the door for Alice. Noah emerged on his side. The car sat on a point near the edge of a sheer cliff with the sea spread out beyond. He could hear the waves on the rocks below. He caught her eye over the roof of the car. "It's beautiful here."

She grinned as though she'd created the setting herself. "I thought you might like it. There's a path down to a fine little slice of beach. A private beach. Is there a blanket or two in the boot?"

There were two. Talbot got them from the trunk. He handed them to Noah and then got back in behind the wheel to wait until they were ready to go.

She'd left her wrap and bag in the car, but her gold sandals had high, delicate heels. Noah eyed them doubtfully. "Are you sure you can make it down a steep trail in those?"

"Good point." She slipped off the flimsy shoes, opened the car door again, and tossed them inside. "Let's go."

Going barefoot didn't seem like a good idea to him. "Alice. Be realistic. You'll cut up your feet."

She waved a hand. "The trail is narrow and steep, yes, but not rocky. I'll be fine." She gathered her gold skirts and took the lead.

The woman amazed him. She led the way without once stumbling, without a single complaint. Halfway down they came out on a little wooden landing with a rail. They stood at the rail together, the breeze off the sea cool and sweet, the dark sky starless, the moon sunk almost to the edge of the horizon now, sending out a trail of shifting light across the water toward the shore.

She said, "We all, my brothers and sisters and me, used to come here together, with my mother and father, when we were children. The observation point above, where we left the car, belongs to my family. The only way down is this trail. The high rocks jut out on either side of the beach, so intruders can't trek in along the shoreline. We've always kept it private. Just for our family, a place to be like other families out for a day by the sea."

"Beautiful," he said. He was looking at her.

She waved a hand, the diamond cuff she wore catching light even in the darkness, sparkling. "But of course, now and then, the paparazzi fly over and get pictures from the air." She sounded a little sad about that. But then she sent him a conspiratorial glance. "Come on." And she turned to take the wooden stairs that led the rest of the way down.

The beach was sandy. He took off his shoes and socks and rolled his trouser legs. They spread one of the blankets midway between the cliffs and the water and sat there together. The breeze seemed chilly now that they were sitting still, so he wrapped the other blanket around her bare shoulders. He put his arm around her and she settled against him as she had in the car, as though she belonged there. For a while they stared out at the moon trail on the water.

Eventually, she broke the companionable silence. "I think I like you too much."

He pressed his lips to her hair. "Don't stop."

She chuckled. "Liking you—or talking?"

"Either."

She laughed again. And then complained, "You're much too attractive."

"I'll try to be uglier."

"But that's not all. You're also funny and irreverent and a little bit dangerous. And a heartbreaker, too, just like Dami said. I really need to remember that and not go making a fool of myself over you."

He put a finger under her chin and lifted her face to him. "I have no intention of breaking your heart. Ever."

She wrinkled her fine nose at him. "I didn't say you would *intend* to do it. Men like you don't go out to hurt women on purpose. They simply get bored and move on and leave a trail of shattered hearts behind them."

He was starting to get a little defensive. "From what I've heard, you've broken a heart or two yourself in the past."

She groaned. "I should have known you would say that. After all, I have no secrets. My whole life is available, with pictures, *lots* of pictures, in the pages of the *National Enquirer* and the *Daily Star*." And then all at once she was shoving away from him, throwing off the blanket and leaping to her feet.

"Alice. Don't…"

"I'm going wading." She gathered up her gold skirts and ran to the water's edge.

He got up and followed her, taking his time about it. Better to give her a moment or two to calm down.

When he reached her, she was just standing there, the foamy waves lapping her slender feet, holding her skirts out of the way. For a moment they stared out at the water together toward the sinking moon on the far horizon.

Then she confessed, "All right, that was a little bit bitchy. Not to mention over the top. Sorry."

He said nothing, only reached out a hand, caught a loose curl of her hair and tucked it behind her ear. He really liked touching her—and he liked even more that she let him. "I was only saying that we're more or less evenly matched."

"But I don't want to be shattered. I don't want to shatter *you*. I want…" Words seemed to fail her.

He ran a finger down the side of her neck. Living silk, her skin. He drank in her slight shiver at his touch. "You want what?"

She gazed out over the water again. "I want to rip off my dress and dive in. Right here. Right now."

A bolt of heat hit him where it counted. Gruffly, he suggested, "Fine with me. I'll join you."

She let her head drop back and stared up at the dark sky. "I can't."

"There's no one here but the two of us."

She lowered her head and turned to him then. "Oh, Noah. That's the thing. I can never be sure, never be too careful. If someone just happened to be lurking back on the trail with a camera and got a shot of me cavorting naked in the waves with you... Oh, God. My mother would never forgive me." She smiled then, but it was a sad smile. "If the paparazzi caught me in the buff now, I don't think I would forgive *myself,* if you want the truth."

"You're being way too hard on yourself. You know that, right?"

"Maybe. I suppose. It didn't used to bother me much. I used to simply ignore it all. I did what I wanted and if the journos had nothing better to do than to take pictures of me and write silly stories about me, so what? But now, well, I feel differently. I'm sick to death of being the wild one, the ready-for-anything, out-of-control Princess Alice."

He had a good idea of what had pushed her over the line. "The pictures from that pub in Glasgow?"

She winced. "You saw them."

"Yeah."

"My mother was pretty upset over them."

He blew out a slow breath. "I thought they were hot."

"More like a hot mess."

"*Hot* still being the operative word."

She turned fully toward him and studied his face, a

deep look, one that made him slightly uncomfortable. And then she said, "I think I really should go home now."

Uh-uh. Not yet. Not this time.

He reached out. He couldn't stop himself. He wrapped his fingers around the back of her neck and pulled her into him. "Kiss me."

"Oh, Noah…"

"Shh." He took her mouth. She made a reluctant sound low in her throat—but then she softened and kissed him back. When he lifted his head, he said, "I've got to get you away from here."

She gazed up at him, eyes shining, lips slightly swollen from the kiss. "Away from where?"

"Away from Montedoro."

She frowned. "That's not going to happen. Tonight is our last night and—"

He stopped her with a gentle finger on her soft lips. "I don't want this to be our last night. And I don't believe that you do, either."

Her slim shoulders drooped. "Noah. Be realistic."

"But I am. Completely. And my point is, it's a fishbowl here—beautiful, glamorous, but still. A fishbowl. Whatever we do together here, there will be pictures and stories in the tabloid press." Plus, it was way too easy for her to escape him here on her own turf. He needed to get her onto his territory for a change. He went for it. "Come back to California with me tomorrow. Come and stay with me for a while."

She pressed her lips together. "Oh, Noah. I really don't think that would be a good idea."

He wasn't giving up. Ever. "Why not? You'll love it there. And I want to show you my world. I want you to meet Lucy."

"Noah, really. I can't just run off with you. Didn't I just explain all this? I'm trying to be more…discreet. Trying to behave myself for a change. Trying to stop throwing myself blindly into crazy situations."

"It's not crazy. The Santa Barbara area is a beautiful place, almost as beautiful as Montedoro. And my stables are world-class. You can ride every day."

"Oh, Noah…" She pulled away from him then. He wanted to grab her and hold her to him, but he knew better. She spun on her heel and raced back up the beach to the blanket again.

He forced himself to stay behind, turning back to the water, staring out at the horizon for a while, giving them both a few minutes to settle down.

When he felt that he could deal calmly and reasonably, he turned to her once more. She sat on the blanket, the other blanket wrapped around her, her knees drawn up, staring at him with equal parts misery and defiance.

He stuck his hands into his pockets and went to her, stopping at the edge of the blanket, not sure what to do or say next.

She tipped her face up to him and demanded, "What are you after, Noah, really? What in the world do you want from me? Because if I'm just another of your conquests, no thank you. I'm not looking for a meaningless hookup right now."

He knew then that he had to go for it, to tell her everything. What else could he do? A clever lie would never satisfy her. "You're not 'just another' anything. You never could be."

"Please don't flatter me."

"I'm not. Will you listen? Will you let me explain?"

He waited for her nod before he said, "I've done damn well for myself."

"Yes, you have. But what does that have to do with—"

"Just go with me here. Let me play this out."

She hugged her drawn-up knees a little tighter. "All right. I'm listening."

"I've done well for myself and I'm proud. Too proud, I suppose. But that's how it is."

She guided a few windblown strands of hair away from that mouth he couldn't stop wanting to kiss. "Yes, well, I get that."

"A few years ago I decided it was about time I got married and founded my dynasty."

"Ah. Of course. Your dynasty." She made a wry little face.

He forged on. "To found a dynasty, there has to be… the right wife. Someone young and strong, someone from a large family, for a higher likelihood of fertility."

She made a scoffing sound. "I don't believe you just said that."

"Believe it. It's true—and here's where my pride comes in. I decided I wanted a princess. A real one."

Her mouth dropped open. "Oh. You are so bad. Incorrigible, really."

He didn't disagree with her. "How do you think I've got as far as I have in life? Not through good behavior and political correctness. I decide what I want and I go after it."

"You know this makes you look reprehensible, right?"

He only gazed down at her, unflinching. "Do you want the truth from me or not?"

She fiddled with the blanket a little and then hitched up her chin. "Yes. I do. Go on."

He continued, "So I started looking. I wanted a special kind of princess, a princess who was different from the rest. No one inbred. Someone beautiful and exciting. If I'm going to be with a woman for the rest of my life, she will damn well *not* be boring—and my kids won't be stupid or dull."

She made a small snorting sound. "Or, God forbid, unattractive."

He asked very softly, "Are you getting the picture here, Alice?"

Her mocking look fled. She swallowed. Hard. "You… chose me?"

"Yes, I did. The first picture I saw of you, I knew you were the one. I read about you—everything I could find. All the tacky tabloid stories. The articles in *Dressage Today* and *Practical Horseman*. It really worked for me that you loved horses. I wanted to meet you, to find out if the chemistry might be right—because in the end, I would have to *want* you. And *you* would have to want *me*. So I found a way to approach you by using my connections to meet your brother first. As it turned out, I liked Damien. We got along. I invited him to visit me in California. And after we'd known each other awhile, he suggested I come to Montedoro. Of course, I took him up on that."

"It was part of your plan."

"That's right. Damien invited me and I came to Montedoro and I found a way to meet you—in the palace stables, where you're most at home. I set out to get your attention. And I found out that my original instinct was solid. Every minute I've spent with you has only made me more certain that my choice is the right one."

"Wait a minute."

"What?"

"Are you going to try to tell me that you're in love with me?"

"Would you believe me if I did?"

She studied him for a moment, her head tipped to the side. "So, then. It's just chemistry. Chemistry and your plan."

"That's why I want you to come to Santa Barbara. We need more time together. I want you to give that to me—to *us*."

"Be realistic, Noah. There isn't any *us*."

He scowled at her. "There will be. And you're thinking too much."

"Right. Because I'm not a stupid princess, remember? You wanted one with a brain."

"Damn it, Alice." He dropped to his knees on the blanket before her. She gasped, but at least she didn't scuttle backward to get away from him. "I'm only telling you that you don't have to worry. You're not just some hookup. I will never dump you. I want you to marry me. I want children with you. And I won't change my mind. You're the one that I want, Alice. I want you for my wife."

Alice wasn't really sure what to say to him at that point.

Strangely, she still liked him after his extraordinary confession. She liked him and wanted him even more than before. Which probably said something really awful about her character. She didn't especially mind that he'd picked her out as a horse trader chooses a broodmare, for her good bloodlines, her sterling temperament, her fine health and conformation—and her excellent pedigree.

What she did care about was the truth, that he'd told

her honestly exactly what he was after—and that she believed him.

Should she have been at least a little appalled?

Probably. But she simply wasn't.

Surprised, yes. She'd known that he wanted her—pretty hard to miss that—but it had never occurred to her he might be seeing her as a wife. As a rule, she wasn't the type of woman a man would set out to marry in advance of even knowing her. Her reputation preceded her and most men looked for someone a bit more sedate when it came time to choose a lifelong companion.

"Alice. My God. Will you please say *something?*"

She hugged the blanket around her more tightly. "Well, I'm not sure what to say. Except that I do appreciate your telling me the truth."

"I didn't know what else to do," he grumbled. "There's something way too straightforward about you. I get it, that you want honesty. And I'm willing to give you whatever you want."

"Well. Thanks. I think."

He braced his hands on his thighs and gritted his strong white teeth. "Please come to California with me."

"Oh, I don't think so...."

He swore low, then turned and sat down beside her. Drawing up his knees, he let them drop halfway open and wrapped his big arms around them. He stared at his lean bare feet. "Why the hell not?"

"Because when I get married, it's going to be to a man I love and trust and know I can count on."

"I didn't ask you to marry me. Yet. I just told you what I'm after. Now we need the time for you to *learn* to trust and count on me."

She turned her head and pinned him with an unwavering look. "You keep leaving out love."

He made a low growling sound. "You make me be honest, and then you want me to come on with hearts and flowers."

"No, I don't want you to come on with hearts and flowers. I truly don't. I want you to be exactly who and what you are. I like you. A lot. Too much. I find you smoking hot. If I wasn't trying to be a better person, I would be rolling around naked on this blanket with you right now."

He shut his eyes and hung his golden head. "Great. Tell me in detail what you're *not* going to do with me."

"Stop it." She leaned toward him.

His head shot up and he wrapped his hand around her neck and pulled her close. "Alice…" His eyes burned into hers.

She whispered, "Please don't…."

With slow care, he released her.

They sat for a minute or two without speaking.

And then she tried again. "For me, right now, running off to Santa Barbara with you tomorrow seems like just another crazy harebrained stunt. I would need a little time to think this over."

He slid her a glance. "So you're not saying no."

"Not yes, either," she warned.

"But you'll think about it."

She nodded. "And you should do some thinking, too—about how you're hoping I'm going to learn to trust and count on you."

He scowled at her. "You're getting at something. Will you just say it, whatever it is?"

"Fine. If we can't talk about love, we can at least talk

about monogamy. Because that's a condition for me. If you ever want me to marry you, your days as a lady-killer are done."

He said very slowly, the words dragging themselves reluctantly out of him, "I haven't been with anyone for months. And I can't believe I'm admitting it to you."

"Good. It's a start." She stood. "I want to go now."

He didn't argue that time. Apparently he agreed that they'd said all they were going to say for one night. He got up, shook out the blanket and tucked it under his arm. She turned and led the way up to the car.

The ride to her villa took only a few minutes. They were very quiet minutes. To Alice it seemed she could cut the silence with a dull knife.

When they pulled up at the curb, she turned to say good-night to him, to thank him for a wonderful evening. Because it *had* been wonderful, even the rockiest parts. Wonderful and true and difficult. And real.

He only reached for her and covered her mouth with his. She swayed against him, sighing, and he wrapped her up tight in his powerful arms.

It was a great kiss, one of the best. So good she almost said yes, she would go with him after all. Anywhere he wanted. To the ends of the earth.

If he would only kiss her like that again.

But instead, she took a card from her jeweled min-audière and pressed it into his hand. "Home and cell. Call me."

Gruffly, he commanded, "Come and stay with me soon."

She leaned close, pressed her cheek to his and whispered, "Noah. Good night." The driver pulled her door open.

She grabbed her shoes and her wrap and jumped out before she could weaken. Then she stood there on the walk, barefoot in her gold dress, and watched his car drive away.

Chapter Five

Noah slept on the plane, but only fitfully. His car and driver were waiting for him at the Santa Barbara Airport when his flight touched down. He'd have one night in his own bed and then in the morning he'd board another plane to San Francisco for meetings with a media firm seeking investors for a TV-streaming start-up.

At the estate, Lucy came running out to greet him. She grabbed him and hugged him and said how she'd missed him. It did him good to see her smile. She seemed to have boundless energy lately. He was pleased at how well she was doing.

They were barely in the front door before she started in on him about college in Manhattan.

He took her by her thin shoulders and held her still. "Lucy."

She looked up at him through those big sweet brown eyes of hers, all innocence. "What?"

"You need to call that school and tell them you won't be attending in the spring."

Her lips thinned to a hard line. "Of course I won't call them. I'm going, one way or another, no matter what."

"Later," he coaxed. "In a year or two, after we're certain you can handle it."

"I *can* handle it. And I'm taking the spring semester. *This* spring semester. You just see if I don't."

Noah tried not to let out a long, weary sigh. She was so completely out there on this—nothing short of obsessed over it. She couldn't go if he didn't write the checks. And he had no intention of allowing her to put her health at risk. "We've been through this. It's too soon."

"No, it's not." She shrugged off his grip. "It's been two years since my last surgery. I am fine. I am *well*. And you know it. It's *not* too soon."

He wanted a stiff drink and dinner and a little peace and quiet before he had to leave again in the morning. He wanted Alice, a lot. But he wasn't going to have her for a while yet, and he understood that. "Please, Lucy. We'll talk more later, all right?"

"But—"

He caught her shoulders again and kissed her forehead. "Later." He said it gently.

She shrugged him off again. "Later to you really means never."

There was no point in arguing anymore over it. Shaking his head, he turned for the stairs.

"I suppose you saw the stories in the *Sun* and the *Daily Mirror.*" Alice sipped her sparkling water and poked at her pasta salad.

It was Saturday, two days since Noah had gone back to America. Rhia had come to Alice's for lunch. The sisters sat in the sunlit breakfast room that looked out on Alice's small patio and garden.

Rhia slathered butter on a croissant. "As tabloid stories go, I thought they were lovely."

"Tabloid stories are never lovely."

"In this case, I beg to differ. The pictures were so romantic. Noah looked so handsome and you looked fabulous. Two gorgeous people out enjoying an evening together at Casino d'Ambre. Totally harmless. Nothing the least tacky. Good press for Montedoro and the casino. And you both seemed to be having such a good time together. I don't see what you're so glum about."

She was glum because she missed him. A lot. It didn't make sense, she kept reminding herself, to miss a man she hardly knew. No matter how smoking hot he happened to be. "I sold him Orion. He arranged to have the veterinarian at the stables yesterday for the prepurchase exam and he's already sent the money." He'd wired the whole amount after the exam, before he got the papers to sign. So very, very Noah.

Rhia swallowed more pasta. "You've changed your mind about parting with the stallion, then, and want to back out of the sale?"

Alice scowled. "Of course not. I'm a horse breeder. I can't keep them all."

"Then what *is* the matter?"

"Everything. Nothing. Did you see the flowers in the big Murano glass vase in the foyer?"

"I did. The vase is fabulous. And the lilies… Your favorite."

"Noah sent them—both the flowers and the vase. He also sent a ridiculously expensive hammered-gold necklace studded with rubies."

"You know, I get the distinct impression that he fancies you." Rhia ate more pasta and chuckled to herself.

"What is so funny?"

"Grumpy, grumpy." Rhia was still chuckling.

"He wants me to come and visit him in California."

"Will you?"

"I haven't decided. He also wants to marry me."

Rhia blinked and swallowed the big bite of croissant she'd just shoved into her mouth. Since she hadn't chewed, she choked a little and had to wash it down with sparkling water. "Well," she said when she could talk again. "That was fast."

"You don't know the half of it."

Rhia set down her glass and sat back in her chair. "I'm listening."

"Oh, Rhia…"

"Just tell me. You'll feel better."

So Alice told her sister about taking Noah to the family beach, about his startling confession that he wanted to marry a princess—Alice, specifically. "Is that insane or what?"

Rhia shrugged. "He's very bold. Just like you. And you've admitted there *is* real attraction between you."

"But don't you think it's wildly arrogant and more than a little strange to decide to marry a princess out of thin air like that?"

"I'm not going to judge him. Please don't ask me to. What I think is that you really like him and lately you're not trusting your own instincts, so you think you *shouldn't* like him."

"Oh, Rhia. I don't know what to do.…"

Her sister gave her a tender, understanding smile. "I think you do. You just haven't admitted it to yourself yet."

Noah arrived home again from the Bay Area on Saturday afternoon.

Lucy did not run out to greet him. Still sulking over

that damn school she wouldn't be going to, no doubt. Fine. Let her sulk. Eventually, she would see reason and accept that she needed more time at home, where he and Hannah, her former foster mom, who managed the estate now, could take care of her. Maybe at dinner that night, if she wasn't too hostile, he could suggest a few online classes. He needed to get her to slow down a little. There was too much stress and responsibility involved in going to college full-time and living on her own. She needed to ease into all that by degrees.

He thought about Alice. On the plane, he'd read the tabloid stories of their night together at Casino d'Ambre. Just looking at the pictures of her in that amazing gold dress made him want to hop another flight back to Montedoro, where he could kiss her and touch her and take off all her clothes.

She should have come home with him. But she hadn't. He had to be patient; he knew it. He was playing the long game with her. And the prize was a lifetime, the two of them, together.

Unfortunately, being patient about Alice wasn't easy. It made him edgy, made him want to pick a fight with someone like he used to do when he was young and stupid—pick a fight and kick some serious ass.

A ride might lift his spirits a little, get his mind off Alice in that gold dress. He put on old jeans and boots and a knit shirt and went out to the stables, where he greeted the staff and chose the Thoroughbred gelding Solitairio to ride.

He took a series of trails that wound over his thirty-acre estate and on and off neighboring properties. His neighbors owned horses, too. They shared an agreement, giving each other riding access.

An hour after he left the stables, he was feeling better about everything. The meetings with the streaming start-up had gone well. Lucy would see the light eventually and agree to take things more slowly. And in time Alice would be his wife.

Sunday, Alice went to breakfast at the palace with the family. She was a little nervous that her mother might not approve of all the press from her night out with Noah.

But Adrienne only greeted Alice with a hug—and congratulated her on getting such a fine price for Orion. Alice was just breathing a sigh of relief when Damien took the chair next to her at the breakfast table.

He leaned close. "So you sold Noah the horse he wanted."

"I did." Alice sipped her coffee.

"Well." Dami spread his napkin on his knee. "Good enough. And now he's gone back to California where he belongs." She promised herself she was not going to become annoyed with her brother, that he only wanted the best for her. Dami added, "And you won't be seeing him again."

That did it. She turned a blinding smile his way. "Actually, he invited me to come and visit him in California."

Her brother didn't miss a beat. "And, of course, you told him no."

"I told him I would think about it. And that is exactly what I'm doing."

Dami gave her a look. His expression remained absolutely calm. But his eyes shot sparks. "Are you *trying* to get hurt?"

She longed to blurt out the rest of it—that Noah wanted to marry her and she just might be considering that, too. But telling Dami was not the same as confiding in Rhia. Rhia didn't judge. Dami had decided he knew what was best for her. "There's no good way to answer that question, and you know it."

Dami only sat there, still wearing *that* look.

She laid it out for him clear as glass. "Mind your own business. Please."

"But, Allie, it *is* my business." He kept his voice carefully low, just between the two of them. "*I* invited him here."

"What is the matter with you?" She spoke very quietly, too. But she wrapped her whisper in a core of steel. "You'd think I was some wide-eyed little baby, unable to take care of myself. You're way out of line about this. You've already told me what you think I need to know. Now you can back off and stay out of it. Please."

"I think I should talk to him. I should have spoken to him earlier."

"Dami. Hear me. Don't you dare."

Something in the way she said that must have finally gotten through to him. Because he shook his head and muttered, "Don't say I didn't warn you...."

"Stay out of it. Are we clear?"

"Fine. We're clear." He was the one who looked away.

The next day, Alice received another vase—Chinese that time, decorated with cherry blossoms and filled with pink lilies, green anthuriums, plumeria the color of rainbow sherbet and flowering purple artichokes. That night he called her.

"I miss you," he said, his voice low and gruff and way too intimate. "When are you coming to see me?"

She felt an enormous smile bloom and couldn't have

stopped it if she'd wanted to. "The flowers are so beautiful."

"Which ones?"

"All of them—the lilies especially. Both vases, too. And that necklace. You shouldn't have sent that necklace."

"Come and visit me. You can wear it for me."

"Thank you. Now stop sending me things."

"I like sending you things. It's fun. How's my stallion?"

"Beautiful. And a gentleman. I hate to part with him."

"You won't have to if you marry me."

"A telephone proposal. How very romantic."

"It wasn't a proposal. Just a statement of fact. You'll know when I'm proposing, I promise you that. I want you to send Orion on Friday—can you do that?"

"Of course. If you have all the arrangements made?"

"I will. He'll fly into JFK, be picked up in a quarantine van and taken to a beautiful little farm in Maryland for testing." The required quarantine for transporting a stallion from Montedoro to the U.S.A. was thirty days, during which time Orion would be tested for contagious equine metritis. "I'll pay a visit to the farm the day after he arrives to see that he's managed the trip well. And I'll arrange to have him put on a hot walker daily for exercise." During quarantine a stallion couldn't be allowed out to pasture or to be ridden. A mechanical hot walker was a machine designed to cool a horse down after exercise. In this case, the machine would give the quarantined stallion the exercise he needed while in isolation.

She said, "By the end of next month, you will have him."

"Come and visit. You can be here when he arrives at his new home."

"That would be a long visit. I do have a life, you know."

He said nothing for a moment. The silence was warm, full of promise. Companionable. "I don't want to take anything away from you. I only want to give you more. We could live here *and* there in Montedoro. I know your work with your horses means everything to you. You wouldn't have to give that up. However you prefer it, that's how it will be."

"Suddenly we're talking about marriage again—but this isn't a proposal, right?"

"Absolutely not. I told you. When I propose, you won't have to ask if that's what I'm doing."

The next night, Tuesday, he called again. She asked about Lucy.

"She's doing well. Feeling great. And still after me to let her move to New York."

"*Let* her? She's twenty-three, you said."

"So? I told you. She hasn't been well for most of her life."

"But, Noah, she's well now, isn't she?"

"She can't be too careful." His voice had turned flat. Uncompromising.

Alice let the subject go. She'd never met Lucy, didn't really understand the situation. She had no right to nag him in any case. They hardly knew each other. She only *felt* as though she knew him. She needed to remember that.

Wednesday, she sent him a text letting him know she'd taken Orion out during her predawn ride.

Hving 2nd thgts abt selling him. He is 2 fabu.

He zipped one right back.

4get it. He's mine.

Hold the tude.

Come 2 C me.

U R 2 relentless.

Rite away wd b gud.

R U NTS?

They went back and forth like that for at least twenty minutes. She stood on the cobblestones outside the stable door, the sun warm on her back, thumbs flying over her phone. It was so much fun.

And yes, she was starting to think that a visit to California might be a lovely idea.

After that day, they texted regularly. He called every night and sent flowers again on Friday, the day Orion boarded a plane in a special stall-like crate for his flight to America.

Noah flew to Maryland to check on his new stallion and then flew from there to Los Angeles for another series of meetings that would go on over the weekend. They kept up an ongoing conversation in text messages, and he called her each night, which rather impressed her. He always called around eight, a perfect time for her since she was sticking close to home and usually at the villa for the evening by then. With the nine-hour time difference, though, it was eleven in the morning in California when he called. Somehow he always managed to call her anyway.

It pleased her, the way he made a point to take the time to get in touch with her consistently. It pleased her a lot. Maybe too much, she kept telling herself.

On Saturday she was expected at a gala charity auction in Cannes. A driver and her favorite bodyguard, Altus, showed up at seven to take her there. It was nice enough as those things went. She bid on several items and visited with people she'd known all her life and had her picture taken with people whose names she couldn't recall. At the end, she wrote a large check for the decorative mirror and antique side table she'd won.

On the drive home, she felt a little down somehow. For some reason, that made her want to talk to Noah. She got out her phone to text him—and it buzzed in her hand.

A text *from* him.

Still @ auction?

That down feeling? Evaporated.

It's over. Cn U tk?

WCU 1 hr.

She was back at her villa when the phone rang. They talked for two hours. She explained how she'd somehow ended up with a mirror and a side table she didn't even want and he told her all about the movie people he'd met with to discuss a film project he was considering investing in. They laughed together and she felt...understood somehow. Connected. And she couldn't help remembering that dream she'd had right after they'd first met, the dream where they rode through a meadow of wild-flowers and talked and laughed together like longtime companions.

Monday, she found pictures of him on the internet. And yes, it was becoming a habit with her, to look him up online. In the pictures, he was having lunch at the Beverly Hills Hotel with a famous movie producer and a couple of actors she recognized. She teased him about it when they talked that night.

He said, "You're checking up on me." He didn't sound the least bothered by the idea. "How am I doing?"

"So far, so good. Not a single scandal since you left Montedoro. No hot gossip about your newest girlfriend."

"You told me I had to be monogamous, remember?"

She half groaned, half laughed. "If you're only sleeping alone because I told you to, you're missing the point."

"Spoken like a woman. Not only does a guy have to do it your way, he has to *like* doing it your way."

"So you're feeling deprived, are you?"

"Only of your company."

She groaned again. "You *are* good. Too, too good."

"Exactly what I keep trying to tell you."

Tuesday, her mother invited her to lunch at the palace in the sovereign's apartment, just the two of them. Alice wondered what she'd done now. But it was lovely anyway to get a little one-on-one time with her mother in the elegant sitting room where Alice and her siblings used to play when they were children.

They chatted about Alice's plans for the stables and her breeding-and-training program, about how happy Rhia and Marcus were. They laughed over how big Alice's nieces and nephews were getting. Her mother had six grandchildren now, seven once Rhia's baby was born. It was hard to believe that Adrienne Bravo-Calabretti was a grandmother so many times over. She remained slim and ageless, her olive skin seeming to glow from within.

"We missed you at Sunday breakfast," Adrienne said a little too casually when they were sharing a dessert of white-chocolate raspberry-truffle cheesecake.

"I had that thing in Cannes Saturday night." And then there'd been that long, lovely chat with Noah. It had been after three when they'd said good-night. "I didn't make it to the stables for my early ride, either. I was…feeling lazy, I guess."

"Dami got me alone and asked for a word with me," her mother said softly. "He's worried about you."

Alice lost her appetite. She set her half-finished cake down on the coffee table. "I'm going to make a real effort not to roll my eyes right now."

Her mother's smile was patient. "Dami loves you. As do I." Alice kept her mouth shut. She couldn't help hoping that this wasn't about Noah after all. Her mother went on, "Your brother is concerned about your relationship with a friend of his."

So much for her hopes. "Oh, really?" Seriously annoyed and unwilling to make a lot of effort to hide it, she laid on the sarcasm. "Which friend is that?"

"The man from California who bought your stallion Orion. Noah Cordell?"

Alice wanted to grab the small cloisonné vase on the coffee table beside their lunch tray and hurl it at the damask-covered wall. "This isn't like you, Mother."

Adrienne had the grace to look chagrined. "You're right. Your father and I have always tried to stay out of the way, to let our children lead their own lives. But your brother was insistent that I speak with you."

"And since Glasgow, you don't trust me."

Adrienne set down her dessert fork. "That's not so."

"I hope not."

"Please, darling. Don't be upset with me."

Alice let out a low sound of real frustration. "I'm not upset with *you*. Not really. But I think I want to strangle Dami. All of a sudden he's worried for my...what? My virtue? It's laughable—besides being more than a little too late."

"Forgive him. He loves you. And I think he's finally growing up. He's changing, starting to think about his life and his future in a serious way, yet not quite sure how to go about making a change."

"Great. Fabulous. Good for him. But what does that have to do with me?"

"He doesn't want you getting hurt by a man who's just like he used to be, a man you met through him."

"He *told* me he would mind his own business. Instead, he came crying to you. And he has no right to bad-mouth Noah. Noah's never done anything Dami hasn't done. Plus, he and Noah are supposed to be friends."

Her mother raised a hand. "It was nothing that bad, I promise you, only that Noah Cordell is a heartbreaker. Dami just doesn't want you to get hurt."

Alice really did want to break something. "I might have to kill him. With my bare hands."

Her mother reached across and clasped her arm, a soothing touch. "My advice? Let it go. On reflection, I honestly do think that this is more about the changes in your brother than anything else." Adrienne tipped her head to the side, considering. "And I think you do like this man, Noah. I think you like him very much."

Alice had nothing to hide. Why not just admit it? She sat a little straighter. "I do like him. I'm beginning to… care for him. He's tough and competitive and way too smart. He calls me every evening. I can talk with him for hours. He's come a long way in his life and he's very proud and more than a little controlling. But he's also tender and funny and generous, too."

Adrienne's expression had softened. "I see that Dami isn't the only one of my children who is changing, growing more thoughtful, more mature, more capable of truly loving— And how about this? I will speak with your brother again on this subject. I will remind him that your life is your own and I have faith in your judgment."

Her mother's words touched her. "Thank you. Noah's invited me to come and visit him in California."

"Will you go?"

"Yes, Mother. I believe that I will."

Chapter Six

That night when Noah called, Alice told him she would like to come for a visit.

He instantly tried to take over. "Come tomorrow. I'll send a plane for you. I'll handle everything."

She was prepared for that. "Thank you. But no. I'll make my own arrangements. I'll need a little more time."

He made a growling sound. "How long is a *little* more time?"

"A couple of days."

"Thursday, then. You're coming Thursday."

"Friday, actually."

"That's three days. You said two."

"It's so nice that you're eager to see me."

"So, then, you'll come Thursday."

Rather than allow him to keep pushing her when she'd already made it clear she would arrive on Friday, she let a moment of silence speak for her.

"Alice. Alice, are you still there?"

"Right here," she answered sweetly.

"I've been patient."

She couldn't suppress a chuckle. "Oh, you have not."

"Yes, I have. I've waited for you to be ready to come to me. Don't you dare change your mind on me now."

"I'm not changing my mind, Noah."

"How long can you stay?"

"A week?"

"Not long enough," he grumbled. "You should stay for a month, at least. Longer. Forever."

"Let's leave it open-ended, why don't we? We'll see how it goes. I'll have to return by the middle of next month for Montedoro's annual Autumn Faire."

"A fair? That sounds like something you could skip this year."

"I never skip the Autumn Faire. There will be a street bazaar and a parade. I'll wear traditional dress and ride one of my horses."

"Sounds thrilling." His tone implied otherwise.

She held her ground. "I have to return for it. I've already agreed to participate."

He relented. "All right, then—and I have a meeting in San Francisco on Friday," he admitted at last. "No way to reschedule it."

"It's not a problem. I can come later, when you're at home."

"But if you came Thursday, you could fly with me up to the Bay Area. We could—"

"Noah."

"What?"

"Just tell me when you'll be back."

"Never mind," he grumbled. "Come Friday. Lucy and Hannah will be here to welcome you. And I'll be home Saturday."

"Wonderful. I'll see you then."

She took Altus and Michelle with her—Altus because her mother insisted that they all use bodyguards when traveling outside the principality. And Michelle because the housekeeper was an excellent companion who never got flustered by long lines or inconveniences and could pack weeks' worth of gear and clothing in a small number of bags.

With the time difference, they were able to leave Nice Friday morning and arrive at Santa Barbara Airport that afternoon. Altus transferred their bags to the car they had waiting and off they went.

It was a short ride along El Camino Real, less than half an hour from the airport to the gates of Noah's property in Carpinteria. The black iron gates parted as the car approached and they rolled along a curving driveway, past vineyards and orange trees and an olive grove, up the gentle slope of a sunlit hill to the white stucco villa with two wings branching off to either side of the carved-limestone entrance.

Even prettier than the pictures Alice had seen of it online, the house was a beautifully simple Italian-style villa, complete with wrought-iron balconies and a red-tile roof. Four wide arches to the left of the entrance framed a front-garden patio centered around a koi pond and landscaped with tropical flowers and miniature palms.

The coffered mahogany door swung open as Altus stopped the car. A slim pixie-haired young woman in skinny jeans, pink Chuck Taylor high-tops and a pink-striped peplum T-shirt bounded out, followed at a more sedate pace by a taller, older woman with thick black hair parted in the middle and pinned up in back.

The girl had to be Lucy, and she looked so eager and happy to have visitors that Alice pushed open her door and called out, "Hello."

"Alice!" The girl blushed. "Er, I mean, Your Highness?"

"Just Alice. Please." She got out of the car and shut the door. "And you must be Lucy...."

"It's so good that you're here." Lucy ran up and embraced her. Laughing, Alice returned the hug. And then Lucy was grabbing her hand and pulling her toward the older woman. "And this is Hannah. Once she was my foster mom, and now she lives with us. She takes care of us—of Noah and me...."

The older woman nodded. "Welcome, Your Highness."

"Thank you, Hannah. Noah's told me about you, about how much he appreciates all you've done for him and Lucy—and call me Alice, won't you?"

"Alice, then," said Hannah with a warm smile. "Let's get you settled. Come this way...."

An hour later, Alice was comfortably installed in a large west-facing bedroom suite that overlooked the estate's equestrian fields and tree-lined riding trails. She could see El Camino Real and the endless blue Pacific beyond that. Michelle and Altus each had smaller rooms above Alice's, on the third floor.

Hannah had provided an afternoon snack of cheese, fresh fruit and iced tea. Alice and Lucy sat on the small balcony off of Alice's room, enjoying the view and the afternoon sun.

Lucy chattered away. "I'm *so* glad you're here. Noah told me all about you, and of course I had heard of you before. Who hasn't heard of your family? It's such a totally romantic story, isn't it? Your mother, the last of her line, visiting Hollywood and falling in love with an actor. I adore the pictures of their wedding, that fabulous dress she wore, all that Brussels lace, the gazillion seed pearls,

the yards and yards of netting and taffeta and tulle...."
Lucy sighed and pressed a hand to her chest. "Oh, my
racing heart. Like something out of a fairy tale." She
plucked a strawberry from the cheese tray and popped
it into her mouth. "And they still love each other, don't
they, your mother and your father?"

"They do, yes. Very much."

"Wonderful. Perfect. Heaven on earth. My mom and
dad were deeply in love, too. But then he died before I
was born. And we lost our mom when I was nine—did
Noah tell you?"

"Yes, he—"

"Ugh! Noah!" Lucy pretended to strangle herself,
complete with the bulging eyes and flapping tongue.
And then she laughed. And then she groaned. "Honestly, I love Noah more than anything, but sometimes I
wonder if he's *ever* going to let me get out on my own. I
used to be sick a lot—he told you that, didn't he? Did he
also bother to tell you I'm *well* now? Hello! I am. And
that I got accepted to the Fashion Institute of Technol-
ogy in New York for the spring semester? I did! FIT
New York. It's the best fashion and design school in the
country. They *loved* my portfolio, and my entry essay
was brilliant, if I do say so myself. But I swear, Noah's
so careful and so sure I can't handle it. I'm afraid that he
won't let me go." She pulled a fat grape off the bunch, ate
it—and kept right on talking. "Noah says you're twenty-
five. Just two years older than me. But you seem so mature, so sophisticated."

Alice smiled at that. "You're making me feel ancient,
you know."

Lucy blinked—and then laughed some more. "Oh,
you're just kidding. I can see that."

Alice wasn't kidding, not really. There was something childlike about Lucy. She came across as much younger than twenty-three. But she didn't seem the least bit ill. On the contrary, she bubbled with energy and glowed with good health. "I'm sure Noah only wants the best for you. But on the other hand, every woman needs to get out and mix it up a little, to make her own way in the world."

"Oh, Alice. That is *exactly* what I keep trying to tell him. I mean, he's done *everything* for me, to make sure I had a chance when I was sick all the time, to get me the best doctors, the most advanced surgeries, the care I needed so I finally got well. I owe him everything, and like I said before, I love him so much. But I *am* well now. And one way or another, I have to make him see that I've got a great chance here. And I'm not passing it up just because he won't quit thinking of me as his sickly baby sister. Do you want to see my portfolio? I'm really ridiculously proud of it."

"I would love to see it."

So Lucy jumped up and ran to get it. She was back, breathless and pink cheeked, in no time. She shoved the cheese tray aside, plunked the zippered case down on the balcony table and started flipping through her designs.

"They're fabulous," said Alice. Because they were. They were very much like Lucy. Fun, lighthearted and brimming with energy. She favored bright colors and she freely mixed flowing fabrics with leather and lace. She had skirts made of netting in neon-bright colors combined with slinky silky tops worn under studded structured jackets. And then there were simpler pieces, too. Everyday pieces. Perfect little dresses, tops that would make a pair of jeans into something special.

Lucy chattered on. "I always loved to draw, you know?

And it was something I could do in bed when I wasn't well enough to go anywhere. I used to make up stories to myself of where I would go and what I would do—*and what I would wear*—when I finally got well. So I started drawing the clothes I saw in my fantasies, the clothes I saw myself wearing. I got Hannah to buy me a sewing machine and I taught myself to sew. I started making those clothes I dreamed of."

"Seriously. These are wonderful. You ought to be on one of those fashion-design shows."

Lucy put her hands over her ears and let out a silent squeal of delight. "Oh, you had better believe it, Alice. One of these days I will, just you watch and see." She flopped back into her chair—and then she sat straight up again. "Oh! I heard all about your beautiful horses, your Akhal-Tekes. I'll bet you want to get out to the stables, huh? Meet the guys and the horses. Ride."

"I would love to ride, but maybe I should wait for Noah." Noah. Just saying his name brought a hot little stab of eagerness to see him again. "He might want to show me around himself."

Lucy beamed. "You are so gone. You know that, right? But it's okay. So is he."

A shiver of pure happiness cascaded through her. "You think?"

"Are you kidding me? He was beyond pissed off that he wouldn't be here when you came. He wanted everything to be perfect for you. And he kept nagging poor Hannah about how it all had to be just so, giving her endless new items for the menus, insisting over and over that there had to be Casablanca lilies in your room, as though Hannah doesn't always remember what he asks for the first time."

Alice glanced through the wide-open French doors at the big vase on the inlaid table in the sitting area. "The lilies are so beautiful, and I do love the fragrance of them."

"Yeah. But he was impossible. Hannah finally had to talk back to him. She hardly ever does that, but when she does, believe me, he listens. She told him to back off her case and not get his boxers in a twist."

"No..."

"Yeah. It was so funny I had to clap my hand over my mouth to keep from laughing out loud—because I'm barely speaking to him lately and if he saw me laughing he would start thinking I was giving in and accepting that I'm not going to New York after all." Lucy lowered her voice then and spoke with steely determination. "But I *am* going. You watch me. One way or another. I'm going no matter what."

A few minutes later Hannah bustled in and shooed Lucy out so that Alice could rest after her long flight. "Dinner at seven-thirty," she told Alice. "It will only be you and Lucy, in the loggia off the family room downstairs. Now, you lie down for a little, why don't you? Put your feet up."

Alice stretched out on the bed, just for a minute or two....

When she woke up, the sun beyond the balcony was half a red-gold ball sinking into the ocean, the sky a hot swirl of orange and purple. The bedside clock said it was quarter of seven. She had a quick shower. When she got out, Michelle was in the bedroom laying out a white dress with a square neckline and a pair of high-heeled red sandals for her.

Alice put on the dress and sandals and went downstairs to the family room off the ultramodern kitchen. The doors were open to the loggia and a table was set for two. Alice sat alone for a few minutes, sipping the iced concoction Hannah had served her, enjoying the fire in the outdoor fireplace that pushed back the slight evening chill, admiring the infinity pool just visible from where she sat and appreciating the expanse of the equestrian fields below.

Eventually, Lucy bounced out to join her, wearing the cutest striped top in mustard and yellow with a pair of cropped black silk pants and high wedge sandals.

"Adorable," said Alice.

Lucy fluttered her lashes and pulled back her chair. "I do my best. You're not so bad yourself." She giggled. "This is nice, isn't it? Just us girls."

"Yes, it is. Very."

"Oh, I knew I would like you. I adore Dami, and I always had a feeling I would get along great with all you Bravo-Calabrettis."

"I didn't realize you knew Dami."

Lucy shrugged. "He's come to stay here several times when he was visiting California. He's always funny and so charming. Right away he insisted that he would just be Dami, not His Highness or anything—the same way you did. I love to talk to him. I could talk to him forever. He takes time, you know, to pay attention to me, even if I am just Noah's little sister."

"You are a lot more than just Noah's sister," Alice chided. "And you're right. Dami *can* be a sweetheart." She'd been so annoyed with him lately she'd lost sight of his good qualities, his lightheartedness and generosity of spirit. She made a mental note to remember the good things about her bossy big brother.

Hannah brought the food and Lucy chattered on. After the meal, Lucy led Alice to the media room, where they shared a bowl of popcorn and laughed over a comedy about four sorority sisters lost in the jungle. It was still pretty early when the movie ended, but Alice couldn't stop yawning. Jet lag had taken its toll. She went upstairs, climbed into bed and was asleep five minutes after switching off the light.

Hours later she woke.

For a moment she didn't know where she was. And then it came to her: Noah's house. The clock by the bed said it was ten after two in the morning. She stared up into the darkness and wondered what had awakened her.

Then she heard a light tap on the door.

And she knew: Noah. She threw back the covers and switched on the lamp as she reached for her robe. Tying the belt as she went, she raced to the door and yanked it wide.

She caught him in the act of raising his hand to knock again. "Noah…" He looked so fine he stole her breath. How could he be even hotter than she had remembered?

"Okay. It's true," he said in that wonderful gruff tone that always made her pulse race. "I caught a midnight flight because I couldn't wait to see you." His gaze ran over her, hot and slow, from the top of her head to the tips of her toes. "You look amazing."

"All squinty eyed and half-asleep, you mean?"

"Exactly."

She scraped her hair out of her eyes and resisted the

urge to launch herself at him. "How long have you been standing out here?"

He braced an arm on the door frame and leaned in close. "About ten minutes, knocking intermittently. I was trying to wake you up without freaking you out."

"Ah. Very...thoughtful."

"You're staring," he whispered, and stared right back.

"Oh, I know. I can't seem to stop. It's just so good to see you." The urge to jump on him and kiss him senseless kept getting stronger.

With slow, deliberate care, he lifted a hand and guided a wild curl of hair off her temple and behind her ear. The light touch struck hot sparks on her skin. "I don't know what's happening to me," he said in a wondering tone. "Standing outside a woman's bedroom door at two in the morning, patiently knocking at measured intervals... It's not really my style."

She yearned to touch him, yet she felt strangely shy. And that had her casting madly about for something at least reasonably intelligent to say. "How did your business meeting go?"

"It was a success." Those blue, blue eyes tempted her down to drowning. And oh, she wanted to go there with him, to sink beneath the waves of shared desire, to lose herself in the heat and hardness of his body. He whispered, "I invested."

"In?"

"A new company. They stream television shows. It's an interesting start-up—though I have to admit, today I could not have cared less. I had a hell of a time concentrating in the meetings. I kept thinking that you were on your way and then, in the afternoon, that you must be here. I kept wishing *I* was here. I couldn't get back fast enough." He said the last softly, a little bit desperately. "And why am I telling you all this? It's nothing you really need to know."

"Of course I need to know that you're thinking of me, that you want to be with me," she told him sternly. "It's important that I know."

He chuckled then. "Ah. That's it. I'm telling you because you need to know."

She had no trouble understanding his desperation. She felt it, too. "I'm glad you came back early. Glad that you stood here in the hallway patiently knocking until I heard you and woke up…."

"I love this…." He touched her cheek beside her mouth.

She had no idea what he was talking about. "This… what?"

He made a low disappointed sound. "You frowned. Gone."

And then she knew. She smiled. "Dimples. You love my dimples?"

"There they are…. Yeah." He touched each one, a matched pair of quick, sweet caresses. And then his finger strayed. He tapped the tip of her chin and traced the line of her jaw, raising little shivers of awareness as he went.

"I spent the afternoon and evening with Lucy," she said. Her voice came out sounding husky and a little bit breathless. "I love her already."

"I knew you would."

She shook her head and gently scolded, "You know she's not happy with you right now…."

"She'll get over it."

Alice wasn't so sure. "She seems pretty determined to get going on her own life."

Twin lines formed between his brows. "She's not strong enough yet."

"*She* says that she is."

"Wishful thinking. She's always been a dreamer."

"Noah. I believe her."

"She can be convincing, I'll admit."

"No. Honestly, if I didn't know she'd been sick, I never would have guessed that she spent so much of her childhood in bed."

"That's because she's better, a lot better. And all I want is for her to stay that way, not to push too hard and end up flat on her back again. In time, yes, she'll get out on her own. But at this point, she still needs taking care of. And why are we talking about this right now?"

"Because she matters. Because you love her. Because she has a right to her own life—and I saw her portfolio. She obviously has talent, a great deal of it. How can you ask her to miss her chance?"

"Alice, come on." He'd changed tactics; his voice had turned coaxing and his eyes were soft as a summer sky. He put a finger to her lips. "Enough about Lucy."

Alice longed to say more. But maybe not now. Not in the middle of the night, when he'd flown home on a red-eye just to be with her, when she was so glad to see him she felt like a moonbeam, weightless and silvery, dancing on air.

She reached up and laid her hand on the side of his smooth jaw. He smelled of soap, all fresh and clean. He must have showered before he came to find her. That touched her, the way he cared so much to please her. So much so, evidently, that his housekeeper had gotten fed up with his endless demands and been forced to take him down a peg. "I like Hannah, too."

He turned his head enough to breathe a lovely, warm kiss into the heart of her palm. "She's the best."

She let her touch trail lower and tugged on the collar of his polo shirt. "And did I mention it's *so* good to see you?"

"You did." He leaned closer. His warm breath touched her cheek. "And I have a question...."

"Mmm?"

"If you're that happy to see me, how come you haven't kissed me?"

She wrapped her hand around his neck and pulled him down to her. "You're right. I need to fix that...."

His lips were so close. "Do it." It was a command, one she was only too happy to obey.

Their lips met.

Paradise.

She slid her other arm up to clasp around his neck and he reached out and reeled her in. Her breasts pressed against his hard chest, and oh, my, down against her belly, she felt how much he wanted her.

And it was so good. So right.

She really had missed him. Three weeks since that first day when she had mistaken him for a stable hand. In three weeks he had become...special to her. Important. Almost a necessity. Like air and water and her beautiful horses.

Now that she had him in her arms again, now that she had his mouth on hers, she didn't want to stop kissing him. She didn't want to let him go. She wanted his kiss, his touch, the heat of his body so close to hers.

She wanted everything.

All of him.

Tonight.

He deepened the kiss, wrapping her tighter in his powerful embrace. She pressed her body closer to his heat and his strength.

It wasn't close enough.

With a little moan, she surged up closer still. He took her cue and caught her by the waist, lifting her. She responded instinctively, wrapping her arms and legs around him.

She gasped. He groaned. She was all over him like a fresh coat of paint, and it was marvelous. The hardest, hottest part of him pressed insistently against the soft womanly core of her, with only a few layers of clothing between.

He tore his mouth from hers and his eyes burned down at her, blue fire. "Alice?"

She knew exactly what he was asking. And she knew she wanted to answer yes.

At the same time, she hesitated. The new Alice, the more cautious Alice, nagged at her to put on the brakes.

And the old Alice, the *real* Alice, was having none of that.

How could she call this magic wrong? It *wasn't* wrong.

All right, yes, she did realize that they had a long way to go if they hoped to carve out a slice of forever side by side. She had to know him better, trust him more.

And *he* had to learn to trust *her,* to count on her.

They both had to find a way to reach for each other with open hearts, to be guided by each other, to hold on, to share support, to count on each other when things got rough.

It's too soon. Her wiser self kept after her. *You know*

how you are, always leaping before you look. She needed to be more careful. She needed to keep from getting swept away in the heat of the moment.

But no.

Being more careful was the *last* thing she needed right now. At least, her heart thought so. With every swift, hungry beat, her heart seemed to insist that it wasn't too soon at all.

In the weeks apart, when they'd talked and texted constantly, something had been changing. Being so far away from him had actually brought them closer.

So that now, tonight, when he touched her at last, when she heard his voice so low and tender, something special happened. All her doubts melted to nothing. And she knew a deeper truth.

She knew that it would be wrong to send him back to his own bed. It would be wrong and it would be false.

And cowardly, too.

What was that lovely thing Rhia had said to her?

That she was a bold person, someone who lived by her instincts. Rhia had said that she should stop trying to be otherwise, stop second-guessing and being overly careful, stop working so hard to be someone she wasn't.

"My God." Noah's eyes blazed down at her. His wonderful mouth was swollen from kissing her, his eyes feral with need. "Alice?"

And she did it. She took the plunge, gave him the answer they both longed for. "Yes."

"Alice…" It came out on a groan and he claimed her mouth again, harder and deeper even than before.

She kissed him back. The choice had been made and she was bound to glory in it. She wrapped her legs and arms all the tighter around him, pressing her hips against him, feeling him there, right where she wanted him, tucked so close against the feminine heart of her.

"Alice," he whispered once more, so tenderly now. "Alice…"

And then he carried her over the threshold into the shadowed bedroom, pausing only to kick the door closed before striding straight for the bed.

Chapter Seven

Noah hardly dared to believe.

Now. Tonight. All night.

Alice, in his arms.

They had far too many clothes on. He needed to deal with that. Fast.

And he did. He took her by the waist and lowered her to the rug by the bed, groaning a little at the wonderful friction as her body slid down the front of him until her bare feet took her weight.

She gazed up at him, eyes lazy and hot, soft mouth parted. "Noah…"

He clasped her waist tighter, not wanting to let go, locking her in place. "Do. Not. Move."

She laughed, full-out as always, and husky, too. The sound played over him, making him hungrier, harder. Even more ready than before. She said, "I'm not going anywhere."

"Good." He let go of her and started ripping off his clothes, shirt first. He bent and reached with both fists over his shoulders, gathering the knit material up in a wad, yanking it off and away.

She remained right where he'd put her, looking like an angel in a white robe that seemed spun of silk and cobwebs, her hair wild on her shoulders, her eyes full of promises he fully intended to see that she kept.

He had his zipper down and his trousers dropped when he realized how he'd messed up. A chain of swear words escaped him.

She laughed again. "Oh, come on, Noah. It can't be all *that* bad."

He bent and yanked his pants back up. "I've got to go get condoms," he confessed with a groan.

"Condoms." She looked at him levelly. Calmly. Regally.

He felt like a complete idiot, a dolt of epic proportions. "I'll run all the way to my rooms. I won't be a minute, I swear."

She reached over, pulled open the drawer by the bed and came up with a box of them. "Will these do?"

The woman amazed him. "You brought condoms all the way from Montedoro?"

She tipped up her chin. So proud. So adorable. "I believe it's best to be prepared and responsible. We've had more than one unexpected pregnancy in my family. Those pregnancies ended well, in good marriages and wanted babies. But still, I prefer not to take that chance."

He felt better about everything. "You *were* planning to have sex with me. God. I'm so glad."

Her chin stayed high. "What I *planned* was to be safe *if* I had sex with you."

He wanted to grab her and kiss her senseless, but he had a feeling he'd be better off at that point to fake a little humility. "Yes, ma'am."

She shook the box at him. "Not that I had any intention of using them so soon...."

"Oh, hell, no. Of course you didn't." *And you damn well better not change your mind now.*

Her dimples flashed. He knew then that it would be all right, that she would let him stay with her. That he would have her, hold her, claim her as his own.

Tonight.

She opened the box, took one out and set it on the nightstand. Then she dropped the box back into the drawer and pushed it shut. "Please. Proceed."

And he did. He proceeded the hell out of getting naked fast. When he tossed away his second sock and stood before her in nothing but a little aftershave, she was all softness and sweet, willing woman again.

"Oh, Noah," she whispered, and she stepped in close. She put her hand on his chest, right over his breastbone. "Oh, my…"

He bent and took her mouth. Incredible, the taste of her. No woman ever had tasted so good.

She was a lot more than he'd bargained for when he went looking for his princess. A whole lot more. And he was absolutely fine with that.

He framed her face in his two hands, threading his fingers up into the tangled cloud of her golden-brown hair. And he went on kissing her, feeding off that tender, wet, hot mouth of hers until he was so hard he started worrying he might lose it just standing there naked at the side of the bed, his mouth locked with hers.

No way could he let that happen.

He got to work getting her undressed, first tugging the tail on the bow that held her robe together. The silken tie slithered off and down to the rug. And the robe fell open, revealing a lacy copper-colored cami and a pair of very tiny matching tap pants. He pushed the robe off her shoulders. It fell with a soft airy sound, collapsing around their feet.

Then he pushed down the tap pants, taking longer about that than he'd intended to. But the feel of her skin under his palms, the glorious smooth curves of her hips, the long, strong length of her flawless thighs....

He kind of got lost in the sheer beauty of her. What red-blooded man wouldn't?

But eventually, she stepped out of the tap pants, and he took the lacy hem of that little camisole and pulled it up over her head and away.

And that was it. They were both naked.

And she was so beautiful he almost lost it all over again. Not fragile, not Alice. Uh-uh. All woman, and strong, a true horsewoman, with more muscle than most, with shapely arms and round, high breasts, a tight little waist and lean hips. And those legs of hers...

He couldn't wait to have them wrapped around him good and hard again.

He scooped her up and laid her down. She didn't argue, only sighed and pulled him down with her, offering that tender mouth up to him once again. He took what she offered and kissed her, a hard claiming kiss.

And he went on kissing her, letting his hands go exploring, loving the feel of her skin, the lilies-and-musk scent of her, those hot little cries she made when he cupped her breasts and teased at the nipples, when he spread his fingers across her belly and rubbed.

It got to him, got to him good, to imagine that tight stomach of hers softening, slowly going round and then turning hard all over again—with his baby. He wanted that, to watch her get bigger with their child. He'd done what he had to do in his life to care for his sister, to make a place in the world that no one could take from him or anyone he claimed as his.

Now he had that place. He had the power and the money to earn what mattered—and more important, to hold on to what he earned, to mold the future for his children and his children's children. He had enough to offer a woman like this one, enough to make her his. To give her everything.

To keep her safe and happy and having his babies.

He let his hand stray lower. He parted the closely trimmed curls at the top of those beautiful thighs. And he dipped a finger in.

Wet. Hot. Silky.

She cried out against his lips and caught his face in her two hands. "Noah…"

He dipped another finger in. "Like this?"

"Yes," she whispered. And, "Yes," again.

"So soft. Hot…"

"Noah. Oh, Noah…"

He liked that. More than anything. The way she said his name like he counted, like she couldn't any more get enough of him than he could of her, like he really was the man he'd worked so hard to become—and that other guy, too. The one in the old jeans and the battered boots, sweeping out the stable, dreaming of the day he might have something to call his own. She liked that guy, too, even if she'd been pissed off at him for misleading her.

She reached down between them, wrapped her fingers around him. And then she started stroking.

He was sure he would die. And he knew it would be worth it.

Too bad he couldn't last if she kept that up. He had to reach down between them and capture her wrist.

Her eyes flew open. "Too much?"

His answer was a hard groan and another deep, hungry kiss. She wrapped both arms around him and held him so close.

He wanted to taste her, in the heart of her, where she was so hot and wet. But it had been too long for him. He feared he wouldn't last long enough to feel her sweet body all around him.

So he groped for the night table and found the condom. He had it out of the wrapper and down over himself in a matter of seconds, and then he lifted up on his hands to position himself.

She gazed up at him, eyes dazed, mouth so soft and willing. And she ran her hands over him, across his shoulders, down his chest. Slowly, she smiled, a knowing, wicked smile, those dimples of hers making naughty little creases in her velvety cheeks.

And then she got her feet braced somehow and she was turning him—turning *them*. She must have seen that she'd surprised him, because another of those throaty killer laughs escaped her.

He found himself on his back, staring up at her. "What?" he asked in a growl, though he had a pretty good idea of what—and he didn't mind in the least.

"I want to be on top, that's all." She folded those muscular legs to either side of his waist and sat up on him.

"Be my guest," he managed on a groan. The view was amazing. He couldn't resist. He cupped her breasts, teased the tight dusky nipples with his thumbs.

And then she lifted up again. She reached down between them and she took him in her hand.

They both groaned as she lowered her sleek, strong

body down onto him. She did it slowly, drawing it out, making him suffer and clearly loving every minute of it.

He grasped her waist, trying to take a little control, trying not to lose it when they were so close.

But she just kept right on at her own pace, slowly claiming him, surrounding him with her wet heat, her silky softness, owning him, taking him in. It went on forever, and every second he knew that he couldn't hold on, couldn't last a second longer.

And yet, somehow, he did hold on. For that second. And the one after that, and even the one after that.

Until she had him fully within her.

She stilled. He followed her lead, holding himself steady, though his whole body ached with the need to move. He stared up at her and she gazed down at him through another sweet, endless space of time. He knew he would explode.

Finally, when he was past the point where he couldn't take it anymore and yet, through some dark miracle, kept on taking it without losing it after all, she started to lift up again.

He still clasped her waist and he grabbed on hard— and pulled her back down. She moaned at that and let her head fall back. So beautiful, her long slim neck straining, her hair falling over her shoulders, her mouth open in another cry, a silent one.

After that he lost track of everything but the pure, perfect sensation of being held tight inside her. She rocked those hard little hips on him and he rocked with her.

It was forever and only a moment. Light exploded behind his eyes, and then he was reaching for her shoulders, pulling her down onto him, tight and close. He let his hands glide along the fine shape of her slender back to grasp the twin curves of her bottom and he held her good and tight and rocked up hard against her.

She took him, she pushed right back. A shudder claimed her and he knew she was almost there. Inside, she closed and opened on him in rhythmic contractions. She cried out.

That did it. He was so ready, and now she was going over. He didn't have to hold out any longer.

He lifted his head enough to claim her mouth. She opened for him, her tongue sliding over his, welcoming him with a keening little sigh as her body continued to pulse around him.

So good. Exactly right. Doubly joined to her, he kissed her and he let it happen, let his climax rise to meet hers. No stopping it now. It rolled up through the core of him, a long wave of heat and energy, spreading outward so that everything—his body, her body, the whole of the world—seemed to shimmer, to open.

He surged up harder than ever into her, still holding the endless kiss they shared. She breathed his name into his mouth. He drank it. Drank *her,* as the end shuddered over him in a spinning-hot explosion of burning, perfect light.

Curled on her side facing the bedside table, Alice woke from a deep, peaceful sleep.

The clock by the lamp said it was almost ten in the morning. Daylight glowed around the edges of the drawn curtains.

She rolled onto her back and eased a hand out, feeling her way across the sheet to the other side of the bed. Empty. Frowning a little, she turned her head.

Gloriously naked, feet planted wide apart on the

cream-colored rug, Noah lounged in one of the sitting-area chairs, watching her through hooded eyes.

Alarm jangled through her. Was something the matter?

She bounced to a sitting position, instinctively pulling the sheet against her bare breasts, pushing her hair out of her eyes. "Noah, what...?"

He got up and came toward her. Her heart rate spiked. He really was one magnificent-looking man, wide shouldered and broad in the chest, with lean, hard arms, a sculpted belly and sharply muscled legs nicely dusted with burnished gold hair. She found herself staring at the most manly part of him. It really was every bit as breathtaking as the rest of him, even at half-mast.

Halting at the side of the bed, he stood staring down at her.

She blinked up at him, vivid images from the night before flashing through her mind. It had been wonderful. They'd used three of her condoms and made love till near dawn, finally falling asleep wrapped up in each other's arms. "Um. Good morning."

He held out his hand. "Come here."

She frowned, tipped her head to the side and tried to figure out what exactly was going on with him. "Is everything...all right?"

He nodded. He really was looking so very serious. She kept having the feeling that something terrible must have happened. But what?

He prompted, "Take my hand." He still had it outstretched to her.

And she thought of that night at the palace when she'd first learned he wasn't a poverty-stricken stable worker after all, and she'd been so angry with him. He'd offered his hand to her then. And she couldn't bear not to take it, couldn't leave him standing there, reaching out to nothing. She just had to reach back.

She took his hand. His fingers curled around hers, warm and strong and steady. And her heart gave a little lurch of pleasure. Of hope and happiness. "Last night was so beautiful, Noah."

"It was," he said softly. "Let go of the sheet."

Why not? She'd never been all that overly modest, anyway. And he'd seen every inch of her last night. Plus, he was naked, too. They were naked together. A ragged little sigh escaped her as she let the sheet drop. He tugged on her hand. She swung her bare legs over the side of the bed and stood.

"This way...." He led her across the lustrous mahogany floor to the nearest set of French doors, where he released her hand and drew the curtain back.

Morning light burnished the equestrian fields. Several of his men were out working with the horses. A breeze blew the branches of the trees lining the riding trails. Farther out, the ocean was a perfect shade of blue with a rim of white waves rolling onto the sandy ribbon of shoreline.

She turned to Noah again and saw he was watching her. His gaze seemed approving. And possessive. A delicious little shiver ran up the backs of her bare calves. Butterflies got loose in her belly—and her anxiety eased. He wouldn't be looking at her in that sexy, exciting way if he was about to break some awful bit of news to her.

"I'll tell you what's even more beautiful than last night," he said. "You are, Alice. You knock me out...."

A flush of pleasure warmed her cheeks. She breathed easier still. It was definitely not bad news, then. He wouldn't take time to shower her with compliments if he had something terrible to tell her, would he?

Surely not.

So if not bad news, then what?

"Alice." And he dropped to a bare knee right there in front of her—at which point the situation became all too clear. Oh, she should have guessed. She started to speak, but before she could make a sound, he raised his other hand.

Wouldn't you know? There was a ring in it, a stunning marquise-cut solitaire on a platinum band. The giant diamond glittered at her.

She managed to croak out, "Oh, Noah…"

And then he proposed to her, right there on his knees, naked in the morning light.

"I know what I want, Alice. I've known for certain since that first morning I saw you in the flesh, tacking up that golden mare in the palace stables before dawn. I want *you,* Alice. Only you. Now, tomorrow, for the rest of our lives. Let me give you everything, Alice. Marry me. Be my wife."

Chapter Eight

Alice caught that plump lower lip of hers between her teeth. "Noah, I…" The words trailed off.

Not that he needed to hear anymore. He already knew by the tone of her voice and the way she looked down at him, so sweet and regretful, that she wasn't going for it.

"Crap." He stood. No point in kneeling in front of her stark naked if she wasn't going to give in and say yes.

She stared up at him, those gray-blue eyes soft and maybe a little worried—for him. That ticked him off. He didn't want her concern. He wanted *her*. Beside him. For the rest of their lives.

"You're amazing," she said. "I really am crazy for you."

He took her by her silky shoulders and grumbled, "So why aren't you saying yes?"

"Ahem." She went on tiptoe and kissed him—a quick little peck of a kiss. And then she settled back onto her heels again and suggested gently, "Maybe you forgot? A certain four-letter word seems to have gone missing from your proposal."

He scowled down at her. "Fine. I love you, then. I love you madly. All the way to distraction and beyond. You are my shining hope, my only dream of happiness. Marry me, Alice. Say yes."

She put her hand on his chest, the way she had more than once the night before. "I know you have a heart, Noah. I can feel it beating away strong and steady in there."

"What the hell is that supposed to mean?"

"It means I know what I want now, after years of throwing myself wildly into all kinds of iffy situations."

Just like a woman. She knew what she wanted, but she failed to share it with him.

Patiently, he suggested, "And what, exactly, *is* it that you want, Alice?"

"I want it all. I'll have nothing less. I want everything. All that you have. Not only your strength and protection, your fidelity and your hot body and half of everything you own. Not only your brilliant brain and great sense of humor and your otherworldly way with my horses. I want your heart, too. And I know I don't have that yet. And until I do, I won't say yes to you."

"My heart." He sent a weary glance in the direction of the forged-iron fixture overhead.

"Your heart," she repeated with great enthusiasm. "Exactly."

"I'll play along. What about *your* heart?"

"I get yours, you get mine. That's how it works."

He let his lip curl into something that wasn't a smile. "You're being sentimental. It's all just words, what you're talking about."

"Uh-uh. It's not just words. And until you understand that and give me what I want from you, I'm not going to marry you. It's just not going to happen."

He was tempted to shake her until a little good sense fell out. "Alice. Think about it. I've already offered you everything."

"No, you haven't. But you will." She spoke with confidence. Only the slight tightening around her mouth hinted she might have doubts.

He decided to look on the bright side. She hadn't said no. She'd only said *not yet.* Very few deals were ever finalized on the first offer anyway.

And she did look so beautiful, standing there naked in the morning light. Her skin had a golden cast and the scent of lilies swam around him.

He couldn't resist. He stroked her hair. She didn't object. In fact, she stared at him with shining eyes, even let out a sweet, rough little sigh when he ran the back of his finger along the side of her neck.

"You want me," he reminded her, just in case she might be thinking of telling him that last night had been a mistake. "You want me and I want you."

She answered with no hesitation. "Oh, yes. Absolutely."

He touched the pulse in the undercurve of her throat. It beat fast. Yearning. Eager. "I want to marry you. I'm not giving up."

"Of course you're not." She searched his face. Her voice was gentle, almost tender. He realized he wanted her more than ever right then. "I love that about you, Noah. I don't want you to give up."

He slid his fingers around the back of her neck, up into the warm, living fall of her hair. "If you're not going to say yes to my proposal right now, the least you can do is kiss me."

"Oh, I would be only too happy to kiss you."

Enough said. He lowered his mouth to hers. She swayed toward him, sliding her arms up around his neck.

Her body pressed like a brand all along the front of him. He was fully erect in an instant.

He grasped her waist, the way he had at the door last night, and lifted her from the floor. Those fine legs came around him and she linked her ankles at the small of his back.

They groaned in unison.

He carried her that way to the bed, where he paused long enough to set the ring she'd refused on the night-stand. Then he lowered her down to the tangled sheets.

She made no objections. On the contrary, she went on kissing him eagerly, deeply.

He might not have her promise to marry him yet.

But he *was* in her bed.

An hour later, Alice handed him the fabulous ring, kissed him one last time and then sent him to his room to shower and dress. He was barely out the door when someone tapped on it.

Michelle peeked in. "Good morning." Alice had put on her robe while Noah was getting dressed, but the cami and tap pants lay on the bedside rug where he'd dropped them the night before. Michelle bustled over and picked them up. "Breakfast here in the room or…?"

"I'll go down. We'll grab a quick bite and then I'll get my first look at the stables, followed by a long ride and a tour of the property."

Michelle only stood there, holding the bits of satin and lace, a look of bemusement on her face.

Alice held her hands out to the side, palms up. "What?"

"You look positively…glowing."

Glowing. Hmm. She felt well satisfied, certainly. It

had been a wonderful night. But she didn't feel exactly glowing. That would come later, if things went as she hoped they might.

She smiled at Michelle anyway. "Thanks. I'm working on it." And she turned for the bathroom and a nice hot shower.

"What's going on?" Alice asked Noah when she joined him at the table out in the loggia. Beyond the open French doors to the family room, men and women in white shirts and black trousers bustled back and forth. A big bearded fellow in a chef's hat had taken over the kitchen. Alice had seen the pots bubbling on the giant red-knobbed steel range. It all smelled wonderful.

"We're having a party," Noah said. "Coffee?" He held the carafe above her cup.

"Yes, please—a party *tonight?*"

"A welcome party for you. Just some people I know— neighbors, business associates. Is that all right with you?"

"Of course. It's only that this is the first time anyone's mentioned a party to me."

"I'm sure they assumed I'd told you. And I should have." He attempted to look contrite. "I'm sorry, Alice."

She laughed then—and she leaned close to him to whisper, "You intended to announce our engagement tonight, didn't you?"

He gave her a dark look and dropped the apologetic act. "You're damn straight. You should say yes and not ruin my big plan."

She sat back in her chair and gazed out at the tree-shaded, sun-dappled garden. "I believe you are the most relentless person I have ever known."

"You're right. I don't give up. You should say yes

now. Telling me no is only putting off the inevitable." He said it teasingly. But he wasn't teasing, not really. Alice thought of the night before, of how sweet and eager he'd been to see her. He had so many stellar qualities. But he did have a ruthless side, a side that demanded loyalty rather than graciously accepting it, a side that strove constantly for control.

He might claim her loyalty. But she ran her own life and made her own choices. And with the man she loved, she would be willing to share control. But never surrender it completely.

"Alice!" Lucy hovered in the open doorway to the family room, wearing a gathered red skirt with white polka dots, a red lace bandeau and a jean jacket with big red buttons. She bounced over, grabbed Alice by the shoulders and planted a big kiss on her cheek. "There you are." She took the chair on Alice's other side, grabbed an apple from the bowl in the center of the table and bit into it with gusto.

Hannah came out carrying two plates piled with scrambled eggs, bacon, browned potatoes and golden toast. "I hope scrambled will do." She set a plate in front of Alice.

"Wonderful." Alice beamed at her and picked up her fork as Hannah set the other plate in front of Noah.

"I had my breakfast *hours* ago," Lucy announced, and chomped on her apple. "So what are you going to do today?" she asked Alice, taking great care to ignore her brother. "I mean, besides partying all night with Noah's rich friends."

Alice reached over and put her hand on Noah's. He turned his hand over and laced his fingers with hers. A delicious little thrill skittered through her. He might be ruthless and overbearing at times, but when he touched her, she couldn't help thinking he was worth it. "Noah is showing me the stables and then we'll go riding."

Lucy waved her half-finished apple. "I would go with you, but I don't think I like the company you keep."

"Lucy." Noah sent her a warning frown.

She continued to pretend he wasn't there. "Well, Alice, I'm going to put in a few hours sketching new designs." She jumped up, bent over Alice and placed an apple-scented kiss on her cheek. "Come find me if he gives you a moment to yourself...."

Noah kept a variety of breeds, including Morgans, Thoroughbreds and Arabians. Each horse was a beauty with impeccable bloodlines, well trained and well cared for. And the stables and facilities were top-notch. None of that surprised Alice, but it was lovely to see it all for herself nonetheless. Orion would be happy here.

She met his staff—the two trainers, the grooms and stable hands—and she admired the dressage and jumping areas, the oval-shaped private racetrack and the state-of-the-art hot walker. Once she'd had the tour, they chose their horses. He rode a big black Thoroughbred mare named Astra and she chose Golden Boy, a handsome palomino gelding with a blaze on his forehead and a thick ivory mane. Altus, on a gray gelding, followed them at a discreet distance.

They rode for hours, on the trails around the property and sometimes onto trails that belonged to his neighbors. The horses seemed familiar with the route and comfortable with drinking from the troughs they came upon now and then along the way.

Eventually, he turned onto a trail that went under the

highway and they ended up at the ocean, on the ribbon of golden beach. It was nearly deserted, which surprised her. As they rode side by side on the wet, packed sand at the edge of the tide, he told her that the beach was privately owned by him and a group of his neighbors.

They rode until they reached the place where the rocky cliffs jutted out into the tide, much like the cliffs at her family's private beach in Montedoro. It was all so beautiful and perfect. Too perfect, really.

It had her thinking of the other Noah, the scruffy down-and-out Noah she'd met first. She wondered about his early years, about his life growing up. Really, she needed to know more about the man he'd started out as.

"Alice."

She glanced over at him. The sun made his hair gleam like the brightest gold. He grinned and her pulse kicked up a notch. Really, the man ought to come with a warning label: Too Hot. Contents Combustible.

He lowered his reins, canting slightly forward. She didn't have to hear him cluck his tongue to know what he was up to.

They took off in unison, her palomino as quick and willing as his black. The wind smelled of salt and sea, cool and sweet as it pulled at her tied-back hair. She bent over Golden Boy's fine strong neck and whispered excited encouragements as they raced toward the other end of the beach, where Altus waited, ever watchful.

The race was too short. They ended up neck and neck—and then turned their mounts as one and raced back the other way.

That time, she won by half a length. But of course, he couldn't leave it. A lucky thing she had that figured out ahead of time. Again they turned and made for the other end.

He had the slightest edge on her and won that time. When they pulled to a halt, he sent her a grin of such triumph she *had* to kiss him. She sidled her mount in close. He must have read her look, because he met her in the middle.

She laughed against his mouth as the horses shifted beneath them, pulling them away from each other—and then bringing them together so their lips met again.

"We need to go back," he told her regretfully. "The party starts at eight."

Side by side, they turned for the trail that would take them beneath the highway and back the way they'd come.

At the stables, they let the hands clean the tack but took care of their mounts themselves. They hosed off all the salt and sand. Then Alice gave Golden Boy a nice long rubdown, while Noah did the same for Astra. A groom led both horses away to feed and water them. Noah had a few things to discuss with the trainers, so she left him and went on to the house, with Altus following close behind.

Lucy must have been watching for her. She was waiting at the side door when Alice approached.

"Come on," she said, and grabbed Alice's hand. "Have a cold drink with me. There's plenty of time...."

So they went up to Lucy's room, which faced the mountains and was as bright and eye-catching as Lucy herself, the linens neon yellow and deep fuchsia pink. There were plants in pots everywhere. Lucy's drawings and designs covered the walls, and a fat orange cat lay on the floor between the open doors to the balcony, sprawled on its back, sound asleep.

Lucy scooped up the big cat and introduced him to Alice. "Boris, this is Alice. I like her a lot, so you'd better be nice to her."

The cat looked exceedingly bored, but Alice said hello anyway and scratched the big fellow behind the ears. She got a faint lazy purr for her efforts.

Lucy got them each a canned soft drink from her minifridge and they took comfy chairs in her small sitting area. It didn't take her long to get around to what was bothering her.

"Lately, I have a hard time remembering how much I love my brother and how good he's been to me," Lucy said in a whisper, as though Noah might be standing out in the hallway, his ear pressed to the door. "I swear, most of the time now I never want to speak to him again. But I know I need to try harder to get through to him before I do anything drastic."

Alice didn't like the sound of that. "Drastic. Like what?"

"You don't want to know."

"But, Lucy—"

"Trust me. It's better if you don't know. It just puts you in the middle of this more than you already are."

"All right, now you're scaring me."

"Oh, please. It's nothing that awful." Lucy knocked back a big gulp of ginger ale. "And I'm twenty-three years old. If I want to walk out of here and not look back, he can't stop me. But I don't want to do that."

"You want your brother's blessing," Alice said gently.

"Yes, I do. And that means I'm going to have to talk to him some more. I'm going to have to try again to get him to see that he has to let me go." She waved a hand. "Oh, not tonight. Not with the big party and all, but tomorrow or the next day. And I know, a minute ago I said you shouldn't be in the middle of this. I do totally get that it's not fair to ask you, but will you maybe just think about backing me up?"

Alice had no idea how to answer. She felt a strong sense of loyalty to Noah. But she also sympathized with Lucy. Noah *was* too protective and Lucy deserved her chance at her dream.

Her indecision must have shown on her face because Lucy groaned. "Okay, never mind. It's not your battle, I know that. Like I said, I shouldn't have asked."

And Alice found herself offering limply, "I'll…do what I can."

Lucy jumped from her chair, grabbed Alice's hand and pulled her up into a hug. "Oh, thank you. And whatever happens, I'm so glad you came here—selfishly for me because I like you a lot and you're so easy to talk to. But also for Noah. I'm so glad he found you and I hope you two end up together in, well, you know, that forever kind of way."

Alice eased from Lucy's grip and set her soft drink on the side table next to her chair. Then she took Noah's little sister by the shoulders and gazed into her wide brown eyes. "I can't say for certain yet what will happen between me and your brother. But I *can* say that you are absolutely marvelous."

Lucy giggled. "I try." And then she grew more serious. "I worry about Noah. I do. Before our mom died, he used to be…softer, you know? At least, he always was with me and Mom. I was sick so much and Mom, well, she was so sad all the time. Noah said she missed our dad. I remember him then as so sweet and good to us. He would do anything for us back then."

Alice reminded her, "I think he would do anything for you right now."

Lucy made a scoffing sound. "But you see, the point is, there are things he *can't* do for me, things I need to do for myself."

Alice had to agree. "All right. I see what you mean."

Lucy dropped back into her chair again. She kicked off her shoes, drew up her feet and braced her chin on her knees. "All those years ago? Before Mom died?"

Alice knew she should be getting back to her room to prepare for the evening ahead. Michelle would be waiting, growing impatient. But then again, this right now with Lucy, was a lot more important than primping for a party. She sat down, too. "Tell me."

"Well, Noah also had a wild side then, when I was little."

Alice wasn't surprised. "I believe that."

"Outside the house, he was big trouble. He didn't fit in and he used to get in fights all the time. It got worse as he got older. He didn't make friends easily. He was an outsider. And he never backed down, so every night was fight night. I guess it's kind of a miracle he never got shot. He did get knifed a time or two, though. *That* was really scary. He'd come home all bloody and Mom had to patch him up. He barely graduated high school. And then somehow he got into business college and found this job working for this guy who flipped houses. Mom was pleased he was working and actually getting a little higher education, but every day she worried he'd get kicked out of college for bad grades or lose his job for fighting. She had that sadness inside her, and it got worse because she feared for him, for his drinking, for his being out all night, being out of control. And then we lost her...." Lucy shut her eyes and dropped her forehead down on her knees.

Alice sat in sympathetic silence, hoping that she would go on.

And she did. She lifted her head and straightened her shoulders. She stared toward the open doors to the balcony. "And that was it. After the day Mom died, I don't think he ever got into another fight. He got control of himself scary fast. He started getting straight As at his business school. I never saw him drunk again. I mean, that's good, I know, that he isn't out beating people's heads in, that he's not a drunk. That he's focused and determined and a big success and all that. He's come so far. I get that. I'm proud of him. But he's definitely not as sweet as he used to be back in the day, when it was just us at home. He's not as understanding, not as open-minded." She turned her head, looked at Alice, then. "I've done my best, I promise you, to keep him real, to remind him that he only *thinks* he owns the world. But I really am well now. I'm one of the lucky ones. And I have my own life I have to live, you know?"

"Of course you do...." Alice felt strangely humbled. She'd thought Lucy childlike at first. But today she saw the wisdom in those innocent eyes.

Lucy reached between their chairs and squeezed Alice's arm. "Noah desperately needs a person like you in his life, someone he can't run all over. Someone who isn't the least impressed by his money, someone who really cares about him and who can stand up to him, too."

Alice hardly knew what to say. "You make me sound so much more exemplary than I actually am."

"That's not true. You *are* exemplary. You're the best

thing that's ever happened to my brother, and I only hope he doesn't blow it and not let you into his heart and end up chasing you away."

Chapter Nine

When Alice got back to her room, Michelle was waiting, tapping her foot in irritation. "What am I going to do with you? Is that hay in your hair? The party starts at eight. Have you forgotten?"

Alice didn't even argue. She headed straight for her bath.

She was ready at a quarter of eight, fifteen minutes before the guests were due to start arriving. She followed the sound of music down to the first floor. A quartet was warming up in the wide curve at the bottom of the stairs—a grand piano, bass, drums and a sultry singer in a clinging blue satin dress, her blond hair pinned up on one side with a giant rhinestone clip, her lips cherry red.

Alice had a look around. In the living room, two full bars had been set up, one at either end. The dining room was one fabulous buffet, set out on the long dining table and on each of the giant mahogany sideboards. She moved on to the family room, where the doors were wide-open on the loggia. Outside, there was more food and yet another full bar.

Noah appeared from the foyer. He was looking cool and casual in an open-collared dress shirt and dark trousers.

He swept her with an admiring glance, head to toe and

back again. "You look incredible in that dress and those shoes." She wore a short strapless black cocktail dress, her classic red-soled patent leather Christian Louboutin stilettos and the hammered-gold necklace he'd bought her. He put an arm around her, drew her close and whispered, "So how come all I can think of is getting everything off of you?"

She laughed and leaned against him, the things Lucy had revealed to her earlier foremost in her mind, making her feel tenderly toward him—and sympathetic, too. He'd been through so much and come so very far. She would try to remember to be patient with him. She teased, "I think I'll keep my clothes on, if that's all right with you. At least until the party's over."

He handed her a glass of champagne and offered a toast. "To when the party's over." They touched glasses, sipped and shared a quick champagne-flavored kiss.

The doorbell rang and the party began.

Alice met a whole bunch of handsome, athletic people, most of whose names she promptly forgot. A lot of them were horse lovers. Many knew of her and her family. And she could tell by the gleam in more than one eye that several of them had read of her exploits over the years. Yes, she did feel a bit like Noah's newest acquisition— a famous painting or a champion racehorse brought out and paraded around, yet more proof of Noah Cordell's enormous success.

But she didn't let it get to her. She'd spent too much of her life with people staring at her to become all that upset if they stared at her some more. She didn't let the ogling bother her, only smiled and tried enjoy herself.

Her second cousin, Jonas Bravo, and his wife, Emma, arrived around eight-thirty. It touched Alice that Noah had thought to invite them. She sat out by the infinity pool with them for over an hour, catching up a little. Emma and Jonas enjoyed a great marriage. They loved their four children and they were clearly blissfully happy together. It always made Alice feel good to be around them. They encouraged her to come visit them at their Bel Air estate, Angel's Crest, anytime she could manage it during her stay. She thanked them and promised she would try.

They went back inside together, the three of them. Alice excused herself to mingle with the other guests. She visited with a couple of minor celebrities who lived in the area and chatted with a lovely older lady about the best local beaches and the fine gardens at Mission Santa Barbara. Then she joined Noah, who was talking horses and polo with three of his neighbors. The nearby polo and racquet club was deep into its fall schedule of polo tournaments. After half an hour of that, she excused herself and went upstairs to freshen her lip gloss.

At the top of the stairs stood a tall, attractive fortyish brunette in red silk. "Your Highness. Hello. I'm Jessica Saunders." Jessica had very angry eyes.

Alice was tempted to simply nod and move on past. But she did want to get along with all of Noah's friends. So she paused when she reached the landing and returned Jessica's greeting.

Altus was below her, following her up, staying close as he always did when there were strangers around. She gave him a quick glance and a slight shake of her head to let him know she was fine. He continued the rest of the way up, passing between her and the other woman, stopping farther down the upper hallway, where he could keep her in sight.

Jessica sighed. "Leave it to Noah to bring home royalty." She delicately plucked the cherry from her Manhattan by the stem and popped it into her mouth. Her red lips tipped upward in a smile that managed to be both lazy and aggressive at the same time.

Alice resisted the urge to explain that her family was not strictly considered royal. Montedoro was a principality, not a monarchy. Her mother held a throne, but she didn't wear a crown. It was a distinction most people didn't get, anyway. Plus, in recent generations, with all the media hype, just about anyone with a title could end up mistakenly being called a "royal." So never mind. Let Jessica call her a royal if she wanted to. "Noah didn't 'bring' me here," she said. "I arranged my own transportation, thank you—and the Santa Barbara area is so beautiful. We rode down to the ocean today. It was fabulous."

Jessica was not interested in discussing the scenery. "Slightly, er, tarnished royalty, however. We've all read so *much* about you...."

Alice kept on smiling. "Tarnished? I'm guessing you must have grown up years and years ago, back when women weren't allowed to be as interesting as men."

Jessica took a large sip from her drink. "Humph. Being royalty, *I'm* guessing *you* know about Henry VIII."

"Well, I did see *The Other Boleyn Girl.* I kind of have a thing for Eric Bana, if you must know."

"I only mean, if you think about it, Noah is a little like Henry VIII, isn't he?"

Alice wished she had a drink in her hand. She could toss it into Jessica's handsome, smug face. "Excuse me?"

"Not that he's ever cut off anyone's head. It's only that he becomes bored with his conquests so easily, wouldn't you say?"

Alice gave up trying to play nice. "I'm sorry, Jessica. Could you try being just a little more direct? Are you telling me that you are one of Noah's 'conquests,' and that he dumped you and now you're bitter and out for revenge because he broke your heart?"

Jessica almost choked on her Manhattan. "No, of course not. It's just what I've heard and what I've observed. I'm a *friend,* a neighbor. I have the next estate over to the north."

"You don't behave like a friend."

"I'm only telling you what I've heard."

"Only spreading ugly rumors, you mean—and trying to cause tension between Noah and me."

Jessica huffed. "As I said, *Your Highness,* it was just an observation. There's no need to get hostile."

"Oh, I'm not hostile. I'm merely disgusted. Now, if you'll excuse me, I see no benefit to either of us in continuing this conversation." Alice started walking. She didn't stop until she reached her room. When she glanced back, Jessica was gone and Altus was right where he'd been a moment before, patiently waiting, ever watchful. She gave him a nod and shut the door.

Once alone, she fell back across the bed and stared at the ceiling and slowly smiled. Her mother would have been proud of her. She'd put Jessica Saunders in her place and then some. And she'd done it without causing her usual scene, without so much as raising her voice.

Later, when all the guests had gone home, Noah did what he'd been waiting all day and evening to do. He took off Alice's black dress and her red-soled shoes and made slow love to her. It was even better than the night before.

She cuddled up close to him afterward, and he stroked

her silky, fragrant hair and thought that even if she hadn't agreed to marry him yet, things were going pretty well between them.

Scratch that. Things were going great.

Then she said, "Tell me about Jessica Saunders." Her tone was a little too careful, too neutral.

He wrapped a thick bronze curl around his finger, rubbed it with his thumb and then let it go. "There's nothing to tell. She's always seemed friendly enough. She's a neighbor, a booster of the new Carpinteria hospital— to which I have written more than one large check. She does like her Manhattans, or so I've been told. And she's divorced. I heard she took her ex-husband to the cleaners. He left her for a twenty-year-old dental assistant from Azusa."

"Ouch. I guess that explains the bitterness. At least to a degree. And she was drinking a Manhattan. Maybe she'd had one too many."

"What bitterness?" He took her chin and tipped it up so he could see her eyes. "What happened?"

She wrinkled up her pretty nose as though she smelled something bad. "Jessica caught me on the stairs and told me that you're like Henry VIII. You quickly get bored with your girlfriends and dump them."

"What a bitch. I never realized." He kept his hand under her chin so he could see her eyes as he told her gruffly, "Not bored. Never dumping you—but didn't I tell you that weeks ago, on my last night in Montedoro?"

"You did. And your dumping me or not isn't really what I'm worried about right now."

"Good." He waited. He wasn't sure where this was going, but he already had a feeling it was in the wrong direction.

She asked, "Are you really *friends* with any of the people who came to the party tonight?"

"Not really, no. But I have a good time with several of them. I enjoy their company. Isn't that enough? Do they need to be people I'd take a bullet for?"

She stacked her hands on his chest and braced her chin on them—and didn't answer his question. "It's beautiful here. I love it."

"So, then, why do you sound like you're leading me someplace I'm not going to like?"

She lifted up enough to plant a hard, quick kiss on the edge of his jaw. "I want to know more about you. I want to know *everything* about you."

He scowled up at her. "Why?"

"Noah, come on. You've asked me to marry you."

"Yeah, I have. And in case you've forgotten, you failed to say yes."

"It's not something a person should enter into lightly. We're talking about a lifetime together. *And* about having children."

"Exactly. So when are you going to say yes?"

She puffed out her cheeks with a hard breath. "A woman with any sense at all needs to know everything she can about a man before she says yes."

"You already know me better than anyone else but Lucy—and maybe Hannah."

"I believe that. And still, I don't know you nearly well enough."

He did love her mouth. He loved it even when she was saying things he didn't want to hear. Idly, he rubbed his thumb across those lush, sweetly shaped lips of hers. "Believe me. You know me well enough."

His assurances failed to shut her up. "No, I don't. And

what I'm trying to tell you is that I need to know more. I want you to take me to Los Angeles. I want to see the street you grew up on, the house you used to live in. I want to meet your childhood friends."

That was not going to happen. "Where did you get this idea?"

She bent her head and pressed the sweetest, softest kiss to the center of his chest. "I was talking to Lucy yesterday. She told me a little about how it was for you before your mom died."

He should have known. "Did she tell you that all I did was fight and drink?"

"More or less, yes. But she also said you had a sweeter side then and that you were more open-minded."

He grunted. Of course Lucy would say that he *used* to be sweeter. And maybe it was even true. Being sweet and open-minded had not gotten him what he wanted and needed in life. "I don't *have* any childhood friends, so there's no one there for you to meet."

"That's all right." She laid her head down, her ear against his breastbone. "I still want to see where you grew up."

He eased his fingers under the warm weight of her hair and settled his hand around the back of her neck. He didn't think he could ever get tired of putting his hands on her. It was another of the many things that made her perfect for him. "It's a neighborhood of small older houses, California bungalows and little stucco Spanish-style homes. Nothing special. You'd get nothing out of seeing it."

"Let me be the judge of that." With her index finger, she traced a squiggly pattern along the outside of his arm. It tickled in a very good way. "You can take me to all the places you used to hang out." She sighed, a tender little sound, and snuggled in even closer. "My sister Rhia met her husband in Los Angeles. Rhia was in college at UCLA and Marcus was on some special military fellowship there. They had a favorite hamburger stand." She chuckled to herself. "I want to go to *your* favorite hamburger stand."

He traced a slow path down the bumps of her spine— all the way to those two perfect dimples on either side of her round little bottom. "No, Alice. I'm not taking you there."

She pushed herself up over him and then brought her face down to his, nose to nose. He could smell lilies. Also, sex. Her nipples were like little pink pebbles against his chest. He started getting hard again. She knew it, too. She smiled in that way she had, all woman and all-powerful. "I wasn't asking your permission."

"Listen to me." He cradled the side of her face and gave her his most uncompromising stare. "No."

"You don't intimidate me, Noah. And you don't get to be the only one in control. If you don't go with me, I'll only go without you."

"What in hell did you and Lucy talk about?" he growled against those fine soft lips of hers.

"I'll never tell." She licked him, just stuck out that clever tongue of hers and ran it in a circle around his lips. He got even harder. And then he opened his mouth and sucked her tongue inside.

The kiss was long and wet and wonderful. Before it was over, he'd flipped her onto her back. And once he had her there, well, he had to kiss her everywhere.

She didn't object. She threaded her fingers into his hair and whimpered encouragements, holding him in place against the wet, slick heart of her sex. He kissed her there until she rolled her head on the pillows and whispered his name, the waves of her climax pulsing against his tongue.

He was sure by then that they were done with the subject of the old neighborhood and he was feeling pleased with himself to have so effectively distracted her.

She smiled at him in a dazed and dreamy way and held down her hand. He took the condom from her and smoothly rolled it on. Then he rose up over her. She didn't even try to gain the top position that time. She simply opened to him, soft and giving and welcoming, more woman than any other he'd ever known.

He lost himself in her. It was perfect. Paradise.

And then, sometime later as they drifted toward sleep, with her arms tight around him, her fingers stroking his hair, she whispered, "Tomorrow, then. We can go to East Los Angeles and after that maybe visit Bel Air and see Jonas and Emma and the children."

In the morning, he told her again that they weren't going to East L.A.

She said, "It's all right, Noah. I'll give you a few days to get used to the idea. And eventually, if you keep refusing to go with me, I'll go by myself."

He decided to leave it at that for now. She'd said she would give him a few days. He was hoping that when those days were up, she'd either have seen the light and realized it was a pointless exercise to try to travel backward into his past—or he would have come up with another, better argument to convince her of why there was no need to go.

He left her for his rooms, where he showered and dressed.

When he got downstairs, she was sitting with Lucy out in the loggia. Their heads were together and they were whispering intently.

Then they spotted him.

They straightened away from each other and smiled at him—both of them, Lucy, too.

His sister hadn't granted him a smile in more than three weeks. He knew her so well, knew what that smile meant. She was mounting a new offensive in her campaign to get him to give her the money to go to New York.

Fine. At least she wasn't acting like he didn't exist. Maybe they could work this out. Maybe this time he would be able to get through to her, get her to see that he only wanted what was best for her.

"Noah," Alice said, too sweetly. "Come join us. Hannah is making French toast with raspberries."

He went and sat down and put his napkin in his lap.

Lucy poured him coffee—buttering him up. Definitely.

Hannah came out with the plates full of food.

Lucy waited until he'd had a couple of fortifying bites of his breakfast before she said, "Noah, I want to try one more time to work this out with you, about New York."

He ate another bite of the French toast. Excellent, as always. And then he took a sip of coffee. "Yeah. I think we do need to settle this." He set down his cup and told her sincerely, "You know I want you to be happy." He slid Alice a quick glance. She was concentrating on her breakfast, staying out of it, which he appreciated. He saw the little twitch of a smile at the corner of her mouth, though, the flash of a dimple. She assumed from what he'd just said that he was rethinking his refusal to send Lucy three thousand miles away.

Lucy had known him a lot longer. She regarded him warily. "If you want to settle it, let me have access to my trust fund so I can get an apartment and get ready for the spring semester."

He set down his fork and said gently, "When you're twenty-five, if you're strong enough."

Alice's faint smile had disappeared. She set down her fork, too, and took a slow, thoughtful sip of her coffee.

Lucy said, "I'm strong enough now." She spoke levelly. He could hear the angry undertone in her voice, but she was controlling it.

So far, anyway.

He said, "Listen. Why don't we compromise?"

Lucy cut a bite of French toast and then didn't eat it. "I want to be flexible, Noah. But with you the word *compromise* only means that we'll be doing it *your* way."

"That's not fair."

"It's the truth."

He'd been thinking it over. And he *was* willing to compromise, willing to let her try more than just the online classes he'd been suggesting. He made his new case firmly. "How about this? One year here. At UC Santa Barbara. The School of Art, the College of Creative Studies. Come on. It's UC. It will be challenging and exciting. You'll learn a lot and enjoy yourself. And you can live at home. We'll see how it goes. Then, after two semesters, we can reevaluate, see how you're feeling, see if you're ready to try New York."

From the corner of his eye, he could see the look on Alice's face. It wasn't a happy one. She just didn't understand. Someone had to make sure that his sister was safe. Lucy wouldn't be realistic, so he had to do it for her.

Lucy came right back at him. "I know UCSB is a great school. But it's not FIT New York. I'll only be treading water there, and I have tread water all of my life, Noah. I've always, forever, been waiting—to get better, to be well, to be like everyone else." Tears filmed her big eyes that were just like their mom's.

If only she would face the truth about herself. "But, Lucy, come on. You're not like everyone else. You have to be careful, you have to—"

"No!" Her fisted hand struck the table. Her plate bounced and flatware clattered. "How many times do we have to go over this?"

Damn it, why couldn't she see? He didn't want this fight any more than she did. "Lucy, I—"

"No. Wait. For once, Noah, won't you please just listen to what I keep telling you? Last year I *wanted* to try UC. You said to wait one more year just to be sure I was strong enough. Well, I have waited. I have waited and waited. My doctors have given me their blessing to live a normal life. I keep up with my blood work and exams and stress tests and everything is stable. When I go, it's not like I'm heading off to the ends of the earth. It's New York. Some of the best cardiac doctors in the world are there. I'll get referrals, you know that, the best of the best. I'll keep up with my checkups. I will be fine."

"Lucy. Come on. No."

Her cheeks flushed hot pink. "Just like that, huh? As always. Just *no.*"

He felt like some monster. But he knew he was right and he couldn't back down. "If you would only—"

"Stop. Just stop." Tears pooled in her eyes. Furious,

she dashed them away. "I'm a healthy, normal woman now, Noah. Why can't you see that? Okay, Mom died. And Dad. But that doesn't mean something awful will happen to me, too. Why are you so afraid I'm going to keel over dead if I dare to get out on my own?"

Mom and Dad. Why did she always have to bring up Mom and Dad? And Alice was just sitting there, taking it all in. He should have insisted that he and Lucy do this in private.

He said with slow care, "This has nothing to do with Mom and Dad and you know it."

"Oh, please. Get real. You are lying to yourself and I have no idea how to get you to stop. You *have* to let me go, Noah. I'm all grown up, I'm in good health, and you haven't been my guardian since I turned eighteen. I'm getting the money somehow. One way or another, I'm moving to New York before the start of the spring semester." Lucy shoved back her chair and threw her napkin on the table. "You just watch me and see if I don't." She whirled and took off like a shot.

"Lucy, get back here!"

She didn't glance back, didn't even break stride. She stormed through the open doors to the family room and vanished from sight.

Once she was gone, he picked up his fork again. He ate a couple of bites of his fast-cooling breakfast, chewing slowly and carefully, keeping it calm.

Eventually, he sent a sideways glance at Alice. She caught him at it. Because she was just sitting there watching him. She had her hands in her lap.

He supposed he had to say something. "I'm sorry you had to see that."

She picked up her fork without saying a word—and

then set it back on her plate. "This is the thing, Noah. I happen to agree with Lucy."

What? Now she was going to get on his case, too? "Look, Alice, I don't think you—"

She put up a hand. "No. *You* look. Lucy's a grown woman and she has a right to make her own choices now. You should release her trust fund and help her do what she's always dreamed of doing. Think about it. Try to see it from her viewpoint. Finally, it's her turn to have her own rich, full life. And you just keep telling her no."

He wanted to shout at her to stay out of it, to remind her good and loud that she had no idea what she was talking about. Lucy wasn't *her* sister. But he didn't shout. He had more self-control than that. "Three years ago she was in Cardiac ICU at UCLA Medical Center. She weighed seventy pounds and her lungs were full of fluid. They said she wouldn't make it. They'd said that before. I brought in another specialist with a different approach. She survived, barely."

"That was three years ago. And then she had the surgery that made all the difference, you said."

"Nothing in this life is certain."

"Noah. It's been two years since the surgery. Her doctors say she's fine."

"Do you imagine you're telling me something I don't already know? She needs more time at home. I'm not going to bend on that. I *can't* bend. I have her best interests at heart."

Alice pressed her lips together. For a second he dared to hope she would let it go. But no. "I don't think you were really listening to her. I don't think you see how determined and focused she is, how very much like you she is…."

"Of course I was listening. And I know she's determined."

"If you don't help her, she's going to find a way to get the money somewhere else."

"She's twenty-three with no credit and no job history. No way can she afford to relocate to New York by the first of the year without my help." A really bad thought occurred to him. He pinned the woman next to him with his hardest stare, at the same time way too aware of how much he wanted her, how exactly right she was for him in every way. How sometimes when he looked at her, he found himself thinking that she'd somehow wound herself all around his heart, that he couldn't imagine his life without her in it. But if she betrayed him… "My God. You wouldn't."

She drew in a slow breath. "Don't think I haven't been considering it."

"Damn it." The two inadequate words felt scraped from the depths of him. "Don't do that to me."

And then she sighed, softened. "I won't. I wish I could, but…"

"What?" he demanded.

And her eyes went soft as clouds in a summer sky. "I know you would never forgive me. I don't think I could bear that."

It meant a lot. Everything. To hear her say that. He wanted to grab her in his arms and lift her high and carry her back upstairs to bed.

But he knew she wouldn't go for that. Not now. She might be unwilling to betray him, but she was firmly on Lucy's side about the move to New York.

And when he thought about that, when he thought about his sister, it ruined the mood anyway.

Chapter Ten

After breakfast, Alice went up to check on Lucy.

She tapped on Lucy's door and Lucy called out in a tear-strangled voice, "Go away, Noah! I don't want to talk to you."

"It's only me," Alice said.

A sob, then meekly, "Alice?"

"Come on, Lucy. Let me in."

Swift footsteps on the other side of the door. And then Lucy flung it wide and threw herself into Alice's arms. "Oh, Alice, Alice, what am I going to do?"

Alice took her to the bed and eased her down. She sat beside her and handed her the box of tissues from the nightstand.

Lucy blew her nose and cried some more and kept insisting over and over, "I'm going. I will find a way. He's not going to stop me. I'm not missing my chance...."

Alice put an arm around her and reminded her softly, "He does love you and he thinks he's doing the right thing for you. You know that, right? He loves you so very much."

"Of course I know." Lucy's breath hitched on a hard sob. "Somehow that makes it all worse. That he loves me so much and he's being so stupid and stubborn and wrong...." Another flood of tears poured out.

Alice hugged her close and made soothing noises and stayed with her until the storm of weeping had worn itself out.

"I'm okay now," Lucy said at the end with a sad little sniff.

Alice smoothed her thick, short, brown hair. "I'll stay with you for a while."

"No, really. I mean it. I'm fine. I think I'll pull myself together and go to my workroom. Patterns to cut, hems to turn. Working always cheers me up."

"You sure?"

"Yeah. And thanks." She gave Alice's arm a fond squeeze. "For coming up, for being here."

"Anytime."

Noah and Hannah were sitting side by side at the top of the stairs when Alice came out of Lucy's room.

Hannah got up. "How is she?"

"Not happy."

"I'll talk to her." She went into Lucy's room and quietly shut the door.

Noah reached up a hand to grab the banister and stood. He looked tired suddenly. Older than his thirty-five years. The sight made Alice's heart ache. "I know," he said glumly. "She doesn't want to talk to *me*."

Alice went to him. She wrapped her arms around his waist and laid her head on his broad, warm chest. Slowly, he responded, pulling her closer, resting his cheek against her hair.

She whispered, "I need to go riding. I think we both do."

He made a low noise of agreement, but then just continued to hold her. She lifted her head to look up at him and she remembered that dream of hers, way back at the beginning, before she knew who he really was. The dream of the two of them, longtime companions, riding together, stopping in a meadow of wildflowers just to talk.

Sometimes that seemed an impossible kind of dream. And then, times like now, as he held her at the top of the stairs after all that awfulness with Lucy, she couldn't imagine herself ever being able to leave him.

"Alice..." He bent his golden head and kissed her, a chaste kiss, a warm firm pressure, his lips to hers. "I'll meet you at the stables."

"I won't be long."

He let her go, and she went to her room to change.

Alice let a full week go by without reopening the subject of a visit to his hometown.

It was a lovely week, all in all. They rode every day, long rides on the eucalyptus-shaded trails and sometimes along the quiet private beach where he'd taken her that first day. There were picnics on that beach, just the two of them, with Altus standing watch. They attended a polo tournament at the club.

And they had each night together.

The nights were unforgettable. Alice adored being wrapped up tightly in his arms.

But there were shadows on the sunny expanse of their pleasure in each other. Alice spent time with Lucy, but Lucy would have nothing to do with her brother. She remained determined that somehow she was moving to New York.

And Noah wouldn't hear a word about letting her go. Alice stayed out of it. She'd told Noah how she felt about the situation that Sunday morning at the breakfast table. She wasn't willing to go against him head-to-head and give Lucy the money she needed, so really, she had nothing else to say about the matter. She left it alone.

Three times during that week, she called Rhia and cried on her shoulder—about Noah's unwillingness to let his little sister grow up and escape his well-meaning control. About love in general. Because she was falling in love with Noah.

She wanted to tell him so. But she didn't.

Her love made her more vulnerable to him. And she'd begun to fear that she wanted more from him than he was capable of giving her. He had his own ideas about the way things ought to be and he was never all that willing to be guided by anyone else. How could they have a partnership of equals if he insisted on believing—and behaving as though—he ran the world?

She'd said she would give him a few days to get used to the idea that they were going to his old neighborhood. But then he'd had that awful fight with Lucy and Alice had backed off. She ached for him and she wanted to give the man a break, not to push him too hard. Those few days she'd said she'd give him to think it over went by, and she didn't bring up the subject of visiting his childhood home. She knew he assumed she was letting it go.

Wrong. She was just waiting for the right moment to try again.

One really lovely thing did happen that week.

Thursday morning, early, Dami called. The first words out of his mouth were, "I called to make amends."

Both pleased and surprised, Alice laughed. "Do go on."

He confessed, "Mother accused me of being a pig-headed ass."

"That doesn't sound like Mother."

"Well, of course, she didn't use those words exactly. But she said that she believed I had it all wrong, that not only are you serious about Noah, he cares for you, too. She said that I, of all people, have no right to judge a man just because he's, er, enjoyed the company of a large number of women."

"Don't you just love Mother?"

He laughed then. "Sometimes I find her much too perceptive. Not to mention right. Why does she always have to be so bloody right?"

"It's a gift."

His voice changed, grew more somber. "I'm sorry, Allie. Noah *is* a good man, and I was an idiot. I hope the two of you will be blissfully happy together."

I hope so, too, she thought. She said, "Thank you. And you are forgiven."

"Good. Is Noah there?"

"He is, as a matter of fact." Sitting right there in her bed under the covers with her, his pillow propped against the headboard, same as hers. She caught his eye. He arched a brow.

"Put him on," said Dami.

So she handed Noah the phone and sat back and listened to his end of the conversation. He said yes several times and then, "Believe me, I'm on it." And then he laughed. A *real* laugh.

She knew then that it was okay between the two men and she was glad.

Noah reminded Dami that he was always welcome at the estate. "Come anytime. Now, tomorrow… You know you never have to call. The door's always open. You can see firsthand that I'm taking good care of your sister."

Dami must have asked about Lucy, because Noah said in a carefully neutral tone that Lucy was fine. They started talking about some business deal they were apparently in on together.

Alice shut her eyes then and let her thoughts drift away.

She woke when Noah kissed her.

"Your brother forgives me for seducing you," he whispered against her parted lips. "But he's expecting a wedding, and soon."

She lifted her arms and twined them around his neck. "Nice try. But when I marry you, it won't be because Dami expects it."

"*When* you marry me? I like the sound of that…." He deepened the kiss.

She sighed and surrendered to the sorcery in his touch. The man had his flaws.

But when he made love to her, she had no complaints.

On Sunday night, a week after that big argument with Lucy, when Noah joined her in her bedroom as he did every night, she kissed him once—and then she walked him backward to the bed.

She pushed him down, kicked off the purple flats she was wearing and straddled him.

He laughed. And then he commanded, "Take off your clothes. Do it now."

"In a minute." She bent over him, nose to nose, grasped the collar of his shirt in either hand and said, "I need to talk to you."

A little frown formed between his dark gold brows. "About?"

"The place where you grew up. I want you to take me there tomorrow."

He reached up, wrapped a hand around the back of her neck and kissed her. It was an excellent kiss, as usual. It made her want to go loose and easy, to forget everything but the taste of his mouth, the feel of his hand, warm and firm and exciting, stroking her nape, tangling in her hair.

But that was exactly his plan, and she wasn't falling for it.

She lifted away from him, though he tried at first to hold her close. When he gave in and let her go, she said, "If not tomorrow, then Tuesday. And if you won't come with me Tuesday, just tell me now and Altus and I will go alone."

His eyes had gone flat and his jaw was set. "We already settled this."

"Excuse me. We did not."

"I told you—"

"I remember. You told me no. I said I would go anyway. And I will, Noah. Lucy will give me the address of the house you lived in."

He growled, "Lucy's in on this?"

Gee, this was going so well. She rolled off him and flopped to her back on the bed. "No. I didn't want to get Lucy involved if I didn't have to." She turned her head and met his shadowed eyes. "But I will. If I can't get the information I need from you, I'll ask her. It's that simple."

"You would drag my sister into this?"

"That's a bit strong, don't you think? I wouldn't drag Lucy anywhere. But would I ask her for the address of the house you used to live in? In a heartbeat."

"You're being unreasonable."

Was she? And was she pushing this too far? "Why

don't you want to take me there? Why don't you want me to go there on my own?"

"It's the past. It's got nothing to do with me anymore."

She reached across the space between them to touch his cheek. "I think you're wrong."

He caught her wrist. "Leave it. Please."

It was the *please* that undid her.

And in the end, what was the point of going if he didn't want to take her there, if he didn't want her to go? She would learn nothing about his secret heart by driving alone past some house where he used to live.

She pulled her hand free of his grip and sat up. And for the first time since she'd come to stay with him, she thought of home with real longing. Of her horses, her villa, the life she'd left on hold. Was this whole thing with him just an interlude after all? Just two people trying and slowly failing to be more than a love affair?

"All right," she said wearily. "I give up. If you feel that strongly about it, I won't go."

Tuesday evening after dinner, when Alice was in her room catching up on her email and messaging with Gilbert about various minor issues at the palace stables, she got a call from Emma Bravo.

"Come on out to the house," Emma said in that cute Texas twang of hers, as though she and Jonas and their children lived out on the range somewhere surrounded by tumbleweeds and longhorn cattle instead of at one of the most spectacular estates in the whole of Bel Air. "You and Noah and his sister, too. It's still warm enough for a swim party and a nice barbecue. The weekend is the nicest. We'll have all afternoon. How 'bout Saturday at two?"

Alice said she'd check with Noah and get back to her tomorrow.

Noah came to join her a few minutes later and she told him about Emma's invitation. "She said to bring Lucy, too."

"Sounds great. I'd love to go. Who knows? Lucy might even agree to come along."

"I hope she will."

"You'd better be the one to ask her," he suggested somewhat grimly. "We'll get an automatic no if the invitation comes from me."

"I will ask her."

"Perfect." He pulled her close and kissed her, a slow, delicious kiss.

He'd been so attentive and sweet since two nights before, when she'd agreed to give up the trip to his old neighborhood. Alice tried to enjoy his kiss and not to think that it would always be that way with him, that he would stonewall her until she did what he wanted and then reward her for being such a good girl by treating her like royalty.

Royalty. That was a good one. She chuckled against his mouth.

He broke the kiss and guided a few stray strands of hair away from her lips, his eyes full of heat and tenderness, his expression openly fond. "Share the joke?"

"It's nothing," she lied. And then she kissed him again.

He scooped her up high in his arms and carried her to the bed. They made love for hours. He knew just the things to do to thoroughly satisfy her body.

Too bad he wasn't quite so willing to satisfy her heart.

* * *

Lucy didn't come to the breakfast table the next morning. Ever since the big argument with Noah a week and a half before, she'd been taking the majority of her meals in her room.

Around nine, after they'd eaten and Noah had gone to his study to make some calls, Alice went upstairs to invite Lucy to Emma's barbecue that weekend. Lucy's empty breakfast tray waited on the floor outside her door, where Hannah or one of the day maids would pick it up.

At least she wasn't starving herself, Alice thought with a smile. The only thing left on that tray was a little corner of toast crust. Her door was open a crack. Apparently she hadn't closed it all the way when she set the tray out.

From inside the room, there was a burst of happy laughter. And then, "Oh, I'm so glad…Yes…Oh, I can't tell you…A lot to ask…Hero…And don't blow me off. You *are* a hero and I…" There was more, but Lucy's voice dipped and Alice didn't catch the rest.

By then she'd reached the door. Curiosity got the better of her. Shamelessly, she eavesdropped.

"No. It will be awful. Please," Lucy wheedled. "Why don't we just go, avoid all that?…But I…Well, all right, if you think it's best…Mmm-hmm…" A hard sigh escaped her. "I know, I do, I understand…"

About then Alice reminded herself that she hated eavesdroppers. And now she was one. She tapped on the door and it swung partway inward.

Lucy sat on the bed, a cell phone to her ear. She caught sight of Alice. Her mouth dropped open and her eyes went saucer wide.

No doubt about it. She had a coconspirator on the other end of the line.

A boyfriend, maybe?

Or someone who'd agreed to loan her money for New York?

Lucy pulled herself together and wiped the guilty look off her face. "Alice!" She waved her forward and spoke nervously into the phone again. "Ahem. Yes…Mmm-hmm. That's right. I really have to go." She disconnected the call and set the phone on the nightstand. "Come on in." She patted the spot beside her on the bed.

Alice shut the door and went to sit beside her. "Sorry I interrupted…"

"Oh? What?" Lucy fluttered her hands about. "The call, you mean? It was nothing. Just a friend. What's going on?"

Alice considered asking Lucy the same question. But she hardly knew where or how to begin. And really, she shouldn't have been listening in on Lucy's conversation. "Have you met my cousin Jonas Bravo and his wife, Emma?"

Lucy blinked. "Jonas Bravo, as in the Bravo Billion-aire? The one whose brother was kidnapped by their psycho uncle when he was just a baby?"

"That's the one." Amazing. Even Lucy knew the old story. Jonas's younger brother, Russell, had been nick-named the Bravo Baby. Russell grew up in Oklahoma under a different name, never knowing his real identity until the truth came out years later.

Lucy picked up her cell phone, stared at it for a moment then set it back down. "I've never met them, but Noah knows Jonas Bravo, I think."

"Yes. They've done business together, Noah and

Jonas. Jonas and Emma were here, at the party Saturday before last."

"I didn't meet them. But I only stayed downstairs for an hour or two...."

"Jonas is a great guy. And Emma is a sweetheart. I love her. They have four children, two girls and two boys. I think the eldest is ten or eleven now. And Jonas has an adopted sister, Amanda, who's in her teens. Emma's invited us out to their Bel Air estate for a barbecue and pool party this Saturday afternoon. You're included."

Lucy wore a distant look. Preoccupied. Not quite present. She frowned. "Um. Saturday, you said?"

"That's right. We would leave in time to be there at two."

"We?"

"You, me and Noah...."

Lucy sighed. "I don't think so."

Alice put an arm around her. "Come on. Consider it, won't you? It will be fun."

Lucy pulled away. "No, really. You two go on. I have... a few projects I'm working on. I need to keep focused."

Alice dressed for riding, and she and Altus went to the stables. She was tacking up Golden Boy when Noah came to find her. She told him that she'd talked to Lucy about Saturday.

"Will she come with us?" He looked so hopeful it made her heart ache.

She shook her head. "She said something about the projects she's working on...."

His big shoulders drooped a little. He stuck his hands into his pockets. "She spends her life hunched over that damn sewing machine."

She turned back to Golden Boy and cinched up the saddle. "Well, I saw her breakfast tray. At least there's nothing wrong with her appetite. I swear she licked her plate clean."

Noah laughed at that and didn't seem quite so sad. He saddled a big gelding named Cavalier and they rode up into the mountains for the day.

She didn't tell him about Lucy's mysterious phone call.

Yes, she felt a bit guilty for keeping that from him. But she shouldn't have been listening in anyway. And Lucy had a right to a secret admirer.

But what if she's found someone to pay her way to New York?

Alice doubted it. It would be a lot of money. Several thousand for an apartment and furnishings, living expenses and tuition, fees, books, supplies and whatever else.

But say, just for the sake of argument, that Lucy did have a generous friend who'd agreed to bankroll her dream....

Alice couldn't help thinking that it wouldn't be a bad thing. True, she couldn't bring herself to write the check that Lucy needed, couldn't bring herself to betray Noah's trust. But Lucy *was* her friend. Loyalty counted with Lucy, too.

So Alice kept her mouth shut about the cryptic conversation she'd overheard that morning.

Saturday, Alice and Noah left for Los Angeles early in the morning. They went in one of Noah's limos, Altus in the front seat with the driver.

The drive only took about an hour and a half.

But Alice wanted to play tourist before the barbecue at Angel's Crest. So they drove down Hollywood Boulevard, past Grauman's Chinese and all the gold stars embedded in the sidewalk. And then they went to Beverly Hills and had coffee at the Beverly Hills Hotel. They drove down Sunset and Alice gawked at all the giant billboards advertising movies and rock groups and lawyers to the stars.

They arrived at Jonas and Emma's right at two. The whole family was there. Alice forgot her worries about Lucy. And Noah seemed more relaxed, too. He laughed often and treated her with open affection. They swam and played Marco Polo and water volleyball with the children. And later they all sat down outdoors to heaping plates of Texas-style barbecue.

At seven Emma started herding her children upstairs for their baths. Alice and Noah changed back into their street clothes. Jonas urged them to stay—overnight, if it suited them. The house was bigger than Noah's, with guest rooms to spare.

But Noah squeezed her hand and she understood that he wanted to get back. That was fine with her. They hadn't planned to stay late anyway. Alice went upstairs to tell Emma goodbye. The kids were running around, the girls and the older boy already in their pajamas. The youngest one, Grady, was still splashing in the tub.

Emma embraced her. "You come back soon...."

The children's voices echoed on the upper landing as Alice went down the stairs. Noah was at the door shaking hands with Jonas.

The car waited right outside, the engine running in the warm twilight.

Altus held the door for her. She ducked in as Noah got in on the other side. He put his arm around her.

She leaned against him. "That was fun…."

His lips touched her hair. "Yeah. A good day…."

Alice felt more hopeful than she had in weeks. Noah *was* a good man. And she wanted to be with him.

Most of the time, it felt so right with him, as though she'd known him all her life—or been waiting to know him. He touched some place deep within her heart that no other man ever had.

Alice sighed, settled her head on his shoulder and thought about how every day she fell more in love with him.

Yes, he had a giant blind spot about Lucy, and serious control issues. And he always seemed to keep something of himself apart from her. Even with all that, she wanted what they shared to last.

She snuggled in even closer, breathed in the wonderfully familiar, deliciously exciting scent that belonged only to him and considered just saying it: *I love you, Noah. I love you very much.*

But then he would only start pushing for a yes on the question of marriage.

And she wasn't quite ready to go that far—not yet, anyway.

The driver pulled up at the foot of the wide steps leading to Noah's front door. Someone had parked a black luxury SUV over by the low wall that surrounded the koi pond.

Noah frowned at her. "Were you expecting anyone?"

"No. Maybe a friend of Lucy's?"

His frown only deepened. They got out. Hannah was

waiting in the open doorway, the light from the foyer behind her silhouetting her tall, slim form. They mounted the wide front steps with Altus close behind.

One good look at the older woman's face and Noah demanded, "What's the matter, Hannah?"

The housekeeper spoke quietly. "Prince Damien is here. He and Lucy are waiting for you in the family room. Lucy has informed me that tomorrow the prince is taking her to New York."

Chapter Eleven

Noah hadn't cracked any heads in fourteen full years. But he burned to crack one now: Damien's, to be specific.

Hannah saw his expression and got out of his way. He headed for the family room.

Behind him, Alice tried to slow him down. "Noah, wait. Please...."

He ignored her and kept going, through the foyer, down the hallway, past the kitchen, to the family room, with the heels of Alice's sandals tapping in his wake.

They were there, the two of them, just as Hannah had said they would be, sitting in the soft white chairs in front of the arched windows. Lucy popped to her feet at the sight of him. Dami rose, too, but more slowly.

A chain of obscenities scrolled through Noah's mind. He demanded, "What kind of crap are you pulling here, Damien?"

Alice came up beside him. "Noah. Can you please just settle down?"

He hit her with an icy look. "Are you involved in this?"

She stared at him. "Involved? What are you talking about?"

Lucy spoke up then. "Stop it, Noah. Alice had no idea that I talked Dami into helping me. You just leave her alone."

He whirled on his sister. "Are you out of your mind? You can't just—"

She cut him off with a cry. "Yes, I can, Noah. And I will. Dami has a place I can stay and he's loaning me the money I need."

Noah felt a fury so hot and so total, it seemed that the top of his head might pop off. He swung his attention to Damien. "Why? I don't get it. Because of Alice? This is some sick revenge because I want to marry your sister?"

Dami stood there and looked at him as if *he* was the one who'd gone over the line. "Of course not, you idiot. Don't be ridiculous."

"I ought to..." He took a step toward Damien.

Alice grabbed his arm. "Noah, don't...."

At the same time, Lucy tried to step in front of Dami as if she was going to protect him, all ninety-eight pounds of her. "Stop it, Noah. I mean it. You stop it right now."

"It's all right, Luce," said Damien, and he took her by the shoulders and moved her out of the way. His bodyguard, who'd been standing by the doors to the loggia, stepped closer. Damien signaled the man back.

Lucy insisted, "I *called* him, all right? I called Dami and I begged him to help me. He's my friend, okay?"

Noah made a low scoffing sound. "Oh. Right. Exactly. Prince Damien is such a hero. The Player Prince only wants to be your *friend*."

"He *is* my friend, Noah! He's my friend, and that's all. Just my friend, and a very good one, thank you. And yes, he's a hero, too. Because he knows how much this means to me and he's willing to help me, willing to go up against *you*. He's not blinded like you are, Noah. By fear and by the things that happened years and years ago. He sees me as I am now, not as I used to be, and he knows how long I've waited, for all of my life so far. He knows it's finally time I came into my own. *He* knows that I'm ready." The tears rose, clogging her voice, making those big brown eyes of hers shine too bright.

About then he started feeling like the monster in the room.

Which was insane. Not true. He was the only one here who understood the risk, the only one determined to keep Lucy safe, to make certain she didn't push herself too far and end up at death's door before he could get there and save her.

"Noah." Alice still had hold of his arm. "Can we just sit down, please? Can we just talk this over like civilized adults?"

"Civilized," he growled at her.

But she had his attention now. She gazed steadily up at him, pleading and determined, both at once.

And from behind them, Hannah said, "Do what Alice says, Noah. Sit down. Lucy will be leaving in the morning, one way or another. Now's the time to make your peace with that."

Noah glanced back at her. She stood next to Alice's bodyguard, and she met his gaze, unflinching. He couldn't bear it. He shut his eyes.

And his father's face rose up, laughing, on the morning of the day that he died. Laughing and grabbing his mother for a hug and a kiss, heading off to work like it was any other day, with no idea that he would never be back again.

He shook his head, blinked away the image—but it only got worse. Next he saw his mother lying on the couch in that cramped run-down bungalow they rented after the bank took their house. His mother, her face sickly pale, clammy with fever sweat, her eyes red and dazed looking, insisting that she was fine, there was no problem. No need for a doctor, it was only a little cold....

Alice still held his arm. And she was nudging him, guiding him to a chair.

He dropped into it, feeling disconnected, as if this was all some weird, awful dream. Alice sat beside him. She took his hand and twined her fingers with his. He let her do that, even held on.

Her hand felt solid, her grip sure and strong. At that moment she seemed the only real thing in the room.

Lucy and Damien sat down again, too. Hannah came over from where she hovered by the kitchen and took the last chair.

He heard himself ask Damien, "When you called to apologize to Alice, were you already planning this?"

Damien shook his head. "Lucy called me a couple of days later."

Alice cleared her throat and asked Lucy, "Was that Dami on the phone Wednesday morning, when I came to your room and asked you to come with us to Angel's Crest?"

"Yes, it was," said Lucy proudly.

"What?" He turned accusing eyes on Alice. "You never said a word." He started to pull his hand from hers.

She wouldn't let go. "I was eavesdropping, and it was none of my business. Lucy left the door open a crack or I never would have heard a thing."

"You should have told me," he insisted. He might have been able to stop this madness before it went so far.

"I shouldn't have been listening," she said slowly and clearly, as if maybe he didn't understand English very well. "It was a private conversation."

Lucy chimed in, "Alice kept it to herself because *she* understands that I'm an adult and I have a right to my privacy."

"You damn well don't have the right to go cooking up harebrained schemes that put your life in danger."

"Oh, don't be so dramatic, Noah. My life is not in danger. I'm perfectly fine." She swung her gaze to Damien. "Listen to him, Dami. And you kept telling me I needed to try again to get through to him. Ha. Like that was ever gonna happen."

Noah winced. Was he really that bad? He only wanted her safety, only cared about her well-being.

Dami said gently, "Easy, Luce. Calm down."

Noah swung his gaze on his so-called friend and longed to leap up and punch his lights out. But he stayed in his seat, held on to Alice and reminded himself that he was thirty-five years old and there were better ways to fight than with his fists.

Lucy turned on him again. "At least I finally got Dami to see that *you* were never going to listen to me. I... Well, I admit I just wanted to sneak away, not to have to go through this." She raised both hands as though to indicate the five of them sitting there, the tension so thick it seemed to poison the air. "But Dami said I had to face you. That you had a right to know exactly what was going on."

He sent another furious glance in Damien's direction. The last thing he needed to hear right now was how wise and enlightened Damien was.

Lucy was still talking. "So here we are. Now you know. Dami's flying me to New York. My things are all packed and outside in the car. Our plane leaves at eight in the morning."

Noah just stared at her. His mind seemed to have locked up. He had to stop her. He just couldn't seem to figure out how.

Damien said, "I own an apartment building in NoHo—near Greenwich Village? There's a vacant one-bedroom. Luce will have that."

Alice squeezed his hand and coaxed, "I've been there. It's a lovely old building. And the apartments are roomy, especially by New York standards."

He blinked and looked at her again. "You're all for this, aren't you?" His voice sounded strange, without inflection, to his own ears.

She answered softly but firmly, too, "I think Lucy is ready, yes. If you'll recall, I've been clear on that. But in the end, Noah, it's not what *I* think that matters. And it's not what *you* think, either. It's Lucy's choice. And now she's found a way to make it happen."

Because of your brother, he thought, but decided not to say. Yeah, he could beat the crap out of Damien for letting Lucy talk him into this, for sticking his nose in where it didn't belong. But Lucy was the key here.

And she wasn't budging. He couldn't get through to her.

She was going. There was no protecting her from herself anymore. One way or another, she would go to New York.

And somehow he would have to learn to live with that.

He met Lucy's wary eyes. "All right. If there's no way to stop you, *I'll* take you. Give me a couple of weeks to put things on hold here. We'll go to New York, get you a place, get you settled in, get your new doctors and services lined up. I'll arrange to get you access to your trust fund. I'll—"

Lucy put up a hand. "No. You're not doing that. You don't get to go with me and take *care* of me, Noah. The whole point is that you have to let me go, let me stand on my own at last, let me make a life that works for me."

He did turn on Damien then. He couldn't seem to stop himself. "So what, then? *You're* going to take care of her?"

"Of course he's not!" Lucy cried. "How many times do I have to say it? *I'm* going to take care of me. Dami's only going to take me to New York, show me my new apartment, loan me an embarrassing sum of money and then go back to his own life—which, if you think about it, is way more than enough."

Damien said quietly, "I'll make sure she's safe, Noah. I won't leave until she's settled in."

Alice leaned close to him. She didn't say anything, just held tight and steady on to his hand. Hannah sat silent, too, her brow furrowed.

None of them agreed with him. Not one of them took his side in this. They didn't know what he knew, hadn't seen what he'd seen.

He couldn't deal. Couldn't take it all in. Couldn't come up with a way to get even one of them to see the situation as he saw it. He turned to his sister again. Her wide mouth was set, her gaze unwavering. He accused, "You'll do what you want to do, then, no matter the cost."

"I *have* to do it, Noah."

"That's a lie."

Alice chided, "Noah, don't..."

He pulled his hand free of hers. There was nothing more to say. "This conversation is through." He stood. "Good night." And he turned on his heel.

Alice called after him. "Noah. Please..."

He kept walking. He didn't stop or look back. Through the kitchen, down the hallway to the foyer, up the stairs to his rooms.

He went inside and slammed the door.

Alice winced at the sound of the door slamming upstairs. She wanted only to go up there, to be with him, to try to ease his suffering at least a little bit.

But it seemed wiser for the moment to leave him alone.

Hannah caught her eye and echoed her thoughts, "Give him a little time...."

Lucy worried her lower lip. "I knew this was going to be awful. I was so right."

Dami suggested rather sheepishly, "You could always slow down a bit, give the poor guy a chance to get used to the idea that you're going."

Lucy shot him a startled glance. "Are you backing out on me now?"

"No. But if you want to think it over a little more—"

"I don't. We're going," she said sharply. And then, more softly, "Please?"

Dami shrugged. "Well, that settles that." He stood. "Allie, a few words, just the two of us?"

Alice got up and followed him out to the loggia.

"You probably don't believe this," he said when they were alone in the cool autumn darkness, "but I'm honestly not the least happy about causing all this trouble."

"So, then, why are you doing it?"

He stared off toward the garden. "I've seen her designs, and she's shown me the clothes that she's made. She's so talented. It's wrong to hold her back."

Alice phrased her next question with care. "I have to ask. Lucy says you're her friend and nothing more.

I'm going to be backing both of you up with Noah after you go. If the two of you are more than friends, I need to know the truth."

Dami groaned. And then he swore. "How can you ask me that? Lucy's very sweet. But she's like a child. I've never been attracted to the wide-eyed innocent type."

"She's *not* a child, Dami. In many ways, she's quite mature."

He stuck his hands into his pockets and cast a glance at the distant moon. "Please. I swear to you on my honor as a prince of the blood. Luce and I are friends. That's all." Alice had known him all her life and she could tell when he was hedging. He wasn't. Not this time. "Peace?" He held out his arms to her.

Alice accepted his embrace. When she pulled back, she said ruefully, "I only wish Lucy could have found someone else to come to her rescue."

Dami made a low ironic sort of sound. "Her options were limited. And for more than a year she's been trying to get Noah to give her a little independence. But he's been locked up tight, absolutely sure something awful will happen to her if he lets her get out on her own. In the end, I couldn't *not* help her. She's got a fine opportunity and she doesn't want to let it slip through her fingers. She has to make the break."

Alice wrapped her arms around herself against the slight chill in the air. "Noah might never forgive you. He might never forgive any of us."

"I think you're wrong. He loves his sister. When push finally comes to shove, he's going to accept that Luce is a grown-up and that she's also fully recovered after that last surgery she had. He'll realize that he doesn't have to take care of her anymore. He'll see that her leaving was the right choice."

Alice blew out a hard breath. "All right, he'll forgive Lucy. But will he forgive *you?*"

"I think so." Dami grinned then, that charming world-famous grin of his. "He'll want to get along with me. After all, I'm going to be his brother-in-law."

She elbowed him in the ribs. "I haven't said I'll marry Noah."

"You didn't have to. It's written all over your face when you look at him. And even tonight, with all hell breaking loose, it was obvious every time he glanced your way that he's found the woman for him."

I hope you're right, she thought. But she decided not to say it. As soon as she did, Dami would ask her why she sounded doubtful. And then what would she say?

That she loved Noah but she hadn't told him so, that for some reason, she couldn't bring herself to say the words? That he kept his heart carefully separate at all times. That he wouldn't take her to the place where he'd grown up and that made her feel that she didn't really have his trust.

She wanted to confide in Dami now, but the timing was all wrong. He'd come to take Noah's sister away. He was in much too deep already. He didn't need her crying on his shoulder, revealing things she ought to be discussing with Noah.

Dami took her hand and wrapped her fingers around his arm. "We'd better go in before Luce gets herself into any more trouble."

They returned to the family room, where Hannah and the two bodyguards waited. Alone.

Hannah sent them a smile that was both wise and

weary. "Lucy went upstairs. She said if *you* two could talk things through, she probably ought to make an effort to work it out with Noah."

Noah expected Alice's soft tap on the door. His pride jabbing at him, he started to bark at her to leave him alone. But his heart wouldn't let him do that.

She infuriated and challenged and thrilled and bewildered him by turns. He was angry at her for not having his back with Lucy, for going so far as to keep crucial information from him. She damn well should have told him about that phone call she'd overheard.

And yet at the same time, in a deeper sense, he knew with absolute certainty that she *did* have his back.

From the first, she'd confused the hell out of him. And she continued to do so.

The soft knock came again.

He left off staring blindly out the sitting-area French doors to go and let her in.

But it wasn't Alice.

It was Lucy.

His gut tightened at the sight of her standing there. "What?" He pretty much growled the word at her and then instantly wished he could call it back.

Lucy surprised him. She refused to let his gruffness send her off in a huff. She stared up at him with her lips pressed together and her eyes full of hope and anxiousness. "Look. You're my brother. I love you so much. And you saved my life. Repeatedly. I know that. I get that. I wouldn't be here without you. I owe you everything. I owe it to you to *do* something with this life I have because of you. I know you're afraid for me and you only want the best for me. I just need you to understand that my going *is* the best thing for me. So please, please, can't you just give me your blessing? Can't you just let yourself be okay with it? Can't you just...let me go?"

Let her go....

As he'd had to let their dad go, and then their mom? No. He couldn't do it. He *wouldn't* do it....

"Please, Noah," she said again. "Please."

And the strangest thing happened. He looked into her upturned face and he saw the naked truth.

He'd lost the damn battle. She *was* going. He could get with the program and help in any way she would let him—or he could let his pride win, turn his back on her, shut the door in her face.

And then never be able to forgive himself if anything actually did happen to her if she felt that she couldn't call him for help because he'd sent her away in anger.

He went with the truth instead of his pride. He gave in. "Lucy..." He let his pain and his love for her show on his face. In his voice. "All right. Yes. I get it. You need to go."

"Oh, Noah..." All at once her big eyes brimmed with tears. "See, I knew it. I did. I knew you would come through for me in the end. Because you always do." She threw herself against him.

He caught her and wrapped his arms around her good and tight. She smelled like cherries and Ivory soap and that made him want to hug her all the harder. "Just...be okay, will you? Just stay safe."

"I'll try. And if I ever get worried I'm not going to make it—"

"You'll call me. I'll be there."

"I promise, Noah. I will."

* * *

Alice hoped against hope that Lucy and Noah would come back downstairs together.

She got her wish.

Brother and sister appeared arm in arm and Lucy announced, "It's okay. We worked it out."

Dami said, "Wonderful." He offered his hand to Noah.

And Noah took it. "She still insists on going with you in the morning, but I'll handle her expenses."

"Fair enough."

Then Noah led Lucy away to his study to write her a check, explain about how he would arrange to give her early access to her trust fund, and no doubt provide endless and detailed instructions on any number of important subjects.

Hannah excused herself. Dami and Alice told their bodyguards to call it a night. They sat and chatted for a while about the family, about the goings-on at home. But Dami kept trying not to yawn. Finally, he had to admit he was jet-lagged. He said good-night. He and Lucy would be leaving before dawn.

Alice lingered in the family room, hoping Noah might finish giving last-minute advice to his sister and come and find her. She was feeling a little unsure.

Was he still angry with her for not taking his side about Lucy's leaving? It made little sense that he would be. He'd ended up accepting the inevitable after all. But then there was the phone call she'd overheard. He'd seemed pretty put out with her for not telling him about that.

Seriously, though. At this point, he should be over that, too. Shouldn't he?

She had no idea if he was or not. And it bothered her. A lot.

Everything had happened so fast at the end. Noah had whisked Lucy off to his study without so much as a glance in Alice's direction. Just a look or a quick squeeze of her hand would have done it, let her know that he'd forgiven her, too.

But then, maybe he hadn't.

The minutes dragged by. Hannah asked her if she'd like some tea or a snack. She almost asked for a vodka tonic—and to make it a double.

But drowning her doubts about Noah in alcohol was no kind of solution. She told Hannah good-night and went upstairs, where she considered calling Rhia and decided not to. It would be seven-thirty Sunday morning in Montedoro.

Alice settled on a bubble bath, heavy on the bubbles. The suite had a nice big tub. She filled it and lit the fat white candles waiting on the rim. Then she undressed, pinned her hair up and sank gratefully into the fragrant, bubbly heat.

It felt so good she closed her eyes and drifted. She tried to forget her worries about Noah, to be happy that what had started out so badly had ended up with Lucy and Noah reconciled and Lucy gaining her freedom at last.

"You look so tempting in that tub I could almost forgive you for not telling me about Lucy's plans…."

Noah.

He might be mad at her, but he *had* come to find her. Her pulse pounded swift and hard under her breastbone. Even in the scented heat of the bathwater, goose bumps prickled across her skin.

She let her eyelids drift open. He lounged against the door to the bedroom, watching her, still fully dressed in the tan trousers and knit shirt he'd worn that afternoon.

"Didn't anyone ever teach you to knock before entering a woman's private space?" she asked him lazily, waving her hands in a treading motion under the water, enjoying the heat and the wet and the feeling of floating.

Not to mention the look in his blue eyes as he watched her. She could stare into those eyes forever and never get bored. A heated thrill of pure anticipation shivered up the backs of her knees.

He undid his belt. It made a soft whipping sound as he pulled it through the loops and off. "I knocked. You must not have heard me."

"But that's the point. If I don't answer, you don't get to come in."

He reached over his shoulders and got hold of the back of his shirt, gathering it in his fists the way he always did, pulling it over his head and tossing it aside. "I wanted to see you." He really did look much too amazing with his shirt off. She admired the depth and breadth of his chest, the power in the muscles of his long arms, the hardness of his belly. And the gold hair in a T-shape, trailing on down to heaven.

Hair dusted his forearms, too. She liked to rub it, just run her hand lightly above the surface of his skin and feel the silky, subtle brush of it against her palm.

What were they talking about?

Right. She was getting on his case for coming in without her knowing. "Still, you shouldn't have."

He undid his trousers and ripped the zipper wide, slanting her a devil's glance as he did it. "Do you want me to leave?"

Her breath came a little shaky. "No. Stay. Join me."

The corners of his mouth curved up and the blue of his eyes grew somehow deeper. Darker. A bolt of heat zipped along her spine, sharp and sweet, pooling in her belly, spreading out slowly like honey in a spoon.

"Happy to oblige." He shucked out of his shoes, lifted one foot and then the other to yank off his socks.

"Lucy all set, then?"

He straightened, barefooted, bare chested, still wearing the tan trousers, though his fly gaped wide, revealing silk boxers beneath. His eyes had changed, gone darker still. There was still heat in them, but there was anger, too. "As set as she's going to be. And I mean it. You should have told me about the phone call."

Alice sat up and shook her head. "I made the right choice on that. You won't convince me otherwise, won't make me feel guilty. Lucy's not only your sister. She happens to be my friend, too. That phone conversation was between her and Damien. I shouldn't have listened in. But then when I did, the only right thing to do was to keep what I'd heard to myself."

His gaze tracked her eyes, her lips. Lower. "You're distracting me, all those wet bubbles on your shoulders, shining on your breasts, sliding down over your nipples…."

She leaned back again, resting her head on the tub rim, letting the bubbles cover her. "Better?"

He made a low sound in his throat and shook his head. And then, swiftly and ruthlessly, he shoved down his trousers and kicked them aside. The boxers followed, down and off. He was fully aroused.

And that turned her on. *He* turned her on.

A lot.

The man was pure temptation—and she'd known it from that first day. From the moment he raised his golden head and met her eyes.

Oh, yes.

Temptation. Coming to get her, to stir everything up—her body, her mind, her heart. To lure her from her home and her horses, to wreak havoc on the careful, well-behaved existence she'd been trying to make for herself after the Glasgow incident.

He came to her then, covering the distance between the door and the tub in five long strides, stepping in at the opposite end and lowering himself slowly until the bubbles covered the proof of how much he wanted her.

His leg brushed hers under the water. She felt his foot sliding along the inside of her calf. And higher. "All right. I forgive you for keeping that phone call to yourself."

She suppressed a low moan of pleasure. "I would prefer if you admitted that I did the right thing."

He regarded her lazily. "Sit up. Let me see your breasts again. You can probably get me to admit just about anything." Something in his voice alerted her.

Something ragged. Raw.

"Oh, Noah…" She did sit up.

"Alice." He said her name low. Rough. And he reached for her.

She went to him, up on her knees between his open thighs, bubbles and bathwater sliding between her breasts and over her belly. Capturing his face between her two hands, she gazed down at him, into his seeking eyes. "What is it?"

He searched her face as though she held truths he needed to find. "Tell me that *I* did the right thing tonight."

She lowered her mouth to him and kissed him. Soft. Slow. Up close, even beneath the floral fragrance of the bubble bath, she caught his scent: sunshine and that aftershave she loved. He tasted of mint. "You did the right thing," she whispered. "Absolutely. The *true* thing." She kissed him again. "And Lucy *is* ready. She's going to be fine. Watch and see."

"God, I hope so. And it wasn't what *I* thought was right. I didn't see a choice, that's all."

She smiled against his lips. "But there *was* a choice. You could have refused to give in. You could have turned your back on her because she wouldn't do things your way. But you didn't. You made the better choice, the *bigger* choice."

"The hell I did," he whispered roughly. And then he caught her lower lip between his teeth, tugging a little before letting go. "She'd better be safe, be all right, or I'll—"

"Shh." She kissed the sound onto his parted lips. "You're not running her life anymore. She gets to be a grown-up now. You're only there for backup *if* she asks you for it."

He laughed low, in equal parts amusement and pain. "You know you're scaring the crap out of me, right?"

"I get that, yes. You had too many losses as a child. You had to make a new life from the ground up, with only your brains and your will to guide you. You had to take control of yourself and your life when your mom died, absolute control. Letting go of it now is not your best thing."

He smoothed the last of the bubbles down her spine, over the curves of her bottom, cupping her, pulling her closer. "I can let go of control."

"Ha," she mocked, trying really hard not to let the teasing sound become a moan.

He brought those wonderful hands between them, sliding them up over her rib cage, cupping both breasts, and he whispered, "You don't know what you do to me. *You* get me out of control."

It pleased her to no end to hear him admit that. She could almost start thinking they were finally getting somewhere. "I do?"

"Oh, yeah…."

"Show me." She kissed him as he caressed her, teasing his lips with her tongue until he let her in, let her taste him slow and deep, let her have control of the kiss. And while she was kissing him, she slipped a hand beneath the water and wrapped her fingers around him nice and tight.

He jerked against her touch and groaned into her mouth. "Alice…"

She stroked him, long, slow strokes. And then faster. Harder. He gave in to her, let her push him back to rest his head on the tub rim, let her guide his hands out to either side, let her slide around and ease her legs under him, bringing his hips above the water and the slowly dissolving bubbles.

He kept those big arms widespread, letting her have him, letting her do whatever she wanted. The sounds he made, low and urgent, drove her on.

She tasted him at her leisure, bending close and surrounding him by slow degrees, letting him free, only to take her sweet time licking all along the length of him.

"Please," he groaned. "Alice…"

And she lowered her mouth on him again, all the way down, then slowly up and down and up again, creating a building rhythm, stroking him with her encircling hand at the same time.

He called out her name. And she felt him, under her palm, at the base, pulsing. She lifted—and then took him in all the way. He touched the back of her throat as he came, tasting of salt and sea foam. She swallowed him down.

A moment later, he reached for her, guiding her around by the shoulders until he could pull her in front of him. He wrapped his arms around her and she lay against him. With her back to his broad chest, the slowly cooling water buoying her, it seemed she felt him all around her, yet she floated above him, too.

He pressed his lips to her temple, murmured rough and sweet in her ear, "We're good together. You know that we are."

She chuckled, a husky, easy sound, tipping her head back enough that they could share a quick kiss. "Spoken like a recently satisfied man."

"I'm serious." Gruff. A little bit angry, but in such a tender, urgent way.

"All right. Seriously, then. Yes, I agree with you. We *are* good together. Mostly."

"You have complaints?" He bent and nipped at the wet skin of her shoulder.

She moaned. "At this exact moment? Not one."

"Good." He cupped her breast with one hand and idly, possessively, teased at the nipple. With the other, he touched her belly, spreading his fingers wide beneath her rib cage, pressing down a little, bringing her into closer contact with his body, making her burn for him within. "I don't want anyone but you." His voice was gruff and soft at once. "I honestly don't. I've been with more women than maybe I should have. But no more. I'm true to you. I *will* be true to you. It's not a hardship. It's what I want."

She reached back, needing her hand on him, and clasped his nape. It felt so good just to touch him. "I'm glad. So glad."

He caught her wrist, brought her hand to his lips, kissed the tips of her fingers one by one. "I started out to find myself a princess."

"Yes. I know."

"I was an ass."

She agreed with him. Gently. "Well, yes. You were. A bit."

"But then guess what happened?" He curved his fingers around hers and brought their joined hands down together under the water. "I went looking for what I thought I wanted—and I found so much more. I found you."

All at once, her throat felt tight and her eyes were brimming. And she couldn't stop herself, didn't *want* to stop herself. She went ahead and said exactly what was in her heart. "I love you, Noah." It came out in a whisper. She made herself say it louder, owning it, proudly. "I'm in love with you. *You're* the one that *I* want, too."

And then he was taking her shoulders again, turning her so that she faced him, so she was meeting his eyes. "Marry me." He said it low. With heat and longing and coaxing intensity. "Say you will. Say yes this time. Be my wife."

Chapter Twelve

Alice longed to give him what he wanted, to tell him yes.

She did want to marry him. She wanted that a lot.

But somehow she couldn't say it. She couldn't quite make herself put that yes out there. She couldn't quite open her mouth and give him the answer he was waiting to hear.

Instead, she only stared at him, mute, her body yearning, her heart aching.

Her silence didn't go over well. The hot, hopeful look left his eyes. They turned cool. Hard.

And then he lifted her off him. Firmly guiding her back to her own end of the tub, he gathered his feet under him and stood.

The water sloshed over the rim and splashed onto the thick bath mat as he got out. He grabbed a towel from the linen cart and wrapped it around his waist. Without stopping to pick up his scattered clothes, dripping water, he headed for the door.

She let out a cry. "Noah, please don't go...."

He kept on walking. Two more steps and he was through the doorway, out of her sight.

She waited to hear the outer door open and shut.

When it didn't, she felt a tiny bit less awful.

He wasn't happy with her, but at least he hadn't stormed out. Well, not *all* the way out. He'd stayed in the suite.

She climbed from the tub, reached for another towel from the stack and dried off, giving him a little time to settle down before trying to talk to him again. At the beveled mirrors over the twin sinks, she took down her hair and shook it out on her shoulders. And then, knowing she'd probably stalled as long as she dared, she snagged her light robe from the back of the door, stuck her arms in the sleeves and belted the sash.

He was standing at the French doors, still wearing the towel, staring out at the moonlit equestrian fields when she found him. She approached with care and drew to a halt a few feet from his broad bare back. About then she realized she had no idea what to say.

Apparently he got tired of waiting for her to find her voice. He demanded, without turning, "What do you want from me, Alice? Heavy use of the L-word? My heart on a pike?"

She fell back a step. "You're being cruel."

He whirled on her then. She startled, certain he would raise his voice to her. But no. He drew in a slow breath and spoke in a tone as even and low as it was dangerous. "I don't know what more to say to you, what else to do to prove to you that I want this, you and me. I want it to last and I intend to do my part to see that it does. I want to be your husband. I want us to have children together. When I get old, I want to be looking over at you in the other rocking chair."

What he said was so beautiful. Her arms ached to reach for him. But she knew he would only pull away from her touch. So she brought her hands up and folded them, prayerfully, under her chin. "I want that, too, Noah. I meant what I said. I love you. I do. You mean the world to me. It's only…" With a hard sigh, she let her arms drop to her sides again. "It's been barely more than a month since we met. I think we need more time."

"Speak for yourself. I *know* what I want."

"All right, then. Speaking for myself, *I* need more time."

"How much time?"

"Some. A little. I don't really know. But when you rush me like this, it only makes me more certain I need to slow things down."

His face looked haggard suddenly. "You say that you love me. But you don't trust me."

Again, she wanted to reach out, smooth his brow, to swear that she *did* trust him, that in the end it would be all right. But she kept her arms at her sides and told him quietly, "It's not you I don't trust. Not really. It's…me."

He threw up both hands. "Oh, excellent. Like there's a damn thing I can do to fix that."

"I don't expect you to fix it. There's nothing *to* fix, not really. There's just…" She struggled for the right words. "Honestly, what you did tonight, making your peace with Lucy, finally letting her go when she's the last of your family and you have this ingrained need to keep her close where you can protect her…. Well, that was amazing. That was really, truly something. It showed me that you *can* compromise, that you're not all about winning, about doing what *you* think is right. That when someone you love finally draws the line on you, you'll do what you have to do to keep the connection. Also, I did hear the things you said to me a little while ago, about being true to me, about wanting me for myself, not because I fit some idea you had of the perfect trophy wife—and then what you said just now, about you and me and the rocking chairs. All of it. It's good. It's right."

He ran a hand back through his hair. "Great. I'm wonderful. Amazing. I say the right things to you. I've proved that I'm flexible, willing to give in. You're in love with me. I'm the guy for you. And still, you keep putting me off."

She wrapped her arms around herself. "I'm an impetuous person. I told you that at the first. My sister Rhia says I do best when I go with that, when I follow my instincts. I think she's right—as a rule. But I do have to be careful about saying yes to sharing the rest of my life. Ten years from now, I don't want either of us to look back and wonder why we said *I do.*"

"That's not going to happen. Not for me."

"I have to be sure, too, Noah."

He was silent, watching her. Then he said, "I think I'll sleep in my room tonight." He started to turn.

"Noah."

"What now?"

"Stay. Please." She held out her hand.

He scowled at it—but then, just when she thought he would turn his back on her, he took it. She pulled his arm around behind her nice and snug, stepping up close and resting her head against his bare chest.

"You don't ask much," he muttered against her hair.

She cuddled closer. "I love you, Noah. Let's go to bed."

Noah let her lead him to the bed. But he'd had enough for the night. Enough of stepping back and letting his sister move to Manhattan where he couldn't protect her.

Enough of having Alice turn him down—even though she claimed to love him.

In bed, she cuddled up close the way she liked to do. He wrapped his arms around her—for a while.

But as soon as her breathing grew even and shallow, he eased his arm out from under her head and slept on his side, turned away from her.

In the morning, they were up before dawn to see Lucy and Damien off. He stood on the front steps with Alice on one side and Hannah on the other, waving goodbye as the black SUV drove away.

Once the car was out of sight, Alice turned to him with a brilliant smile, those gorgeous dimples flashing. He made his lips curve upward in response. But his heart wasn't in it.

They spent the day in the stables and out working with the horses. That night, she asked him if something was wrong.

He shook his head and kissed her. They went upstairs together. He'd been thinking that maybe he'd sleep in his own room. But she kissed him again and he couldn't resist her, so that led where it always led.

Later, as they lay together in the dark, she reminded him that she had to leave on Wednesday. "Next weekend is the Autumn Faire, remember?"

He did remember. "The bazaar and the parade you have to ride in."

"That's it." She settled in closer, pressed her lips to his shoulder. "Come with me. It will be fun."

Was it going to go on like this indefinitely, then, with the two of them constantly together in every way except the one that mattered most to him? "I can't."

"Why not?"

"Didn't I tell you? I have a trip to Amarillo Thursday."

She went very still. And then a small sigh escaped her. "No. You didn't tell me."

He *hadn't* told her, and he knew that he hadn't. In fact, the invitation from Yellow Rose Wind and Solar was open-ended. He'd just that moment decided to go on Thursday. "A West Texas wind farm. I want to have a look before I decide how much to invest."

She rolled away from him, sat up and switched on the lamp. "I'll ask you again." She pulled the sheet up to cover her pretty breasts and settled back against the headboard. "What's wrong?"

He started to insist that there was nothing. But instead, he hauled himself up to sit beside her. "Look. It's hard for a guy. To keep asking and getting told no, all right?"

She kind of sagged to the side and put her head on his shoulder, which felt really good, absolutely right. Damn it. "I'm not saying no. I'm just saying not yet."

He couldn't hold back a grunt of disgust. "Sounds a lot like no to me. And then there's the love thing. You said that you love me."

"Because I do." She clasped his upper arm, squeezing a little. He shifted, easing away from her until she let go, lifted her head from his shoulder and frowned at him. "Is there something wrong with my saying I love you?"

He had no idea why they were talking about this. He never should have let it get started. "It's nothing. It doesn't matter."

"Yes, it does. You know it does."

"It's nothing, Alice."

"That's not true."

"Can you just leave it alone?"

She winced. "You mean it bothers you that I told you I love you and then turned down your proposal?"

It occurred to him that if he said yes to that question, this conversation that made him feel as though poisonous spiders were crawling around under his skin might end more quickly. "Yeah. That's it. It ticks me off. You said you love me—and then you refused to marry me."

She leaned in closer, so their noses almost touched. He wanted to push her away—and he wanted to grab her good and tight and bury his face in her sweet-smelling hair. "How about this? I won't say those dreaded words again until I'm ready to answer yes."

He would prefer that she never said them again. Not ever. But if he admitted that, she'd be all over him, wanting to know what was wrong with him that he had such a big issue with the L-word. The questions would be endless. The spiders under his skin would start biting.

Uh-uh. Not going there.

He said, "It's a deal."

She cradled the side of his face, and then combed the hair at his temples with a fond, gentle touch. "Are you worried about Lucy?"

"Hell, yes."

"She's going to be fine, Noah."

"So everyone keeps telling me."

She kissed him. He breathed in her sweetness. "Reschedule your visit to the wind farm," she whispered. "Come to Montedoro with me."

He shook his head. "You go home. I'll go to Texas. We can't be together all of the time."

"Noah." She held his gaze steadily. "Are you trying to get rid of me?"

"Of course not."

She kissed his chin, his jaw and then nipped at his ear. "Say that again."

"I'm not trying to get rid of you."

"Prove it." Her naughty hand slid down beneath the sheet.

A moment later he flipped her over on her back and showed her just how happy he was to have her around.

Lucy called him the next day. He took the call in his study and couldn't help smiling at the breathless, happy sound of her voice.

"Noah! New York is amazing. The energy here... I could work round the clock and never need to sleep. And my apartment! It's in a beautiful old building. I have tall windows facing the street. There's a claw-foot tub in the bathroom and those old black-and-white subway tiles. The building has seven floors, two apartments per floor, except for the top two floors, which are Dami's for when he's in town. Noah, I'm here just a day and I have so many ideas I can't sketch them fast enough."

He chuckled. "Speaking of fast, have you already moved in?"

"No. Remember? I'm at the Ritz-Carlton for the next few days while I get the place furnished and all that— I mean, at least until I get a bed in and a few basics for the kitchen and bath."

"Good, then." He knew she didn't want to hear it, but he had to caution her, "Don't push too hard. Take care of yourself...."

She laughed. "Oh, I will. I promise you. And I'm feeling great. Fabulous. Never better, I swear."

"How's Damien?"

"He's been wonderful. So helpful and sweet. Plus,

he's easy to talk to and I can ask him anything. He never laughs at me for being so inexperienced and having way too many silly questions."

"Is he...there at the hotel with you?"

"Uh-uh. He's staying at his apartment—the one in my new building?"

Excellent. Noah felt relieved enough to tease her. "Right. *Your* building."

"It *is* my building, because I'm going to live there. Tomorrow he's taking me furniture shopping. But then Wednesday he has to go back to Montedoro." Good. Noah was willing to believe that Dami and Lucy were friends and nothing more, but he would still rest easier when the Player Prince had left New York. Lucy added, "Some festival or something."

"The Autumn Faire."

"That's it. He has to drive a race car in a parade. He's been so sweet, though, Noah. He introduced me to nice Mrs. Nichols across the hall from me. And there's a great building superintendent, Mr. Dobronsky. He takes care of the apartments and fixes anything that gets broken. I met him and his wife, Marie, too. I liked them both a lot."

He couldn't help smiling. "You like *everyone* a lot."

"Mostly, yes. I do." She said it proudly. "And how about you?"

"I'm fine. Perfect."

"Hannah?"

"She misses you already."

"I miss her, too. I'll call her tonight. How's Boris holding up?" Hannah would be taking the cat to her later.

"He'll survive."

"And Alice?"

"Good. Alice is good."

Lucy chided, "You'd better *be* good to her."

A curl of annoyance tightened his gut. "Oh, come on, Lucy. Of course I'm good to her."

"You know what I mean. Treat her right. Take care of her. Let *her* take care of you. Don't close yourself off. Don't boss her around."

"Just what I need." He tried to make a joke of it. "Relationship advice from my baby sister."

But Lucy wasn't kidding. "Someone has to say it. Alice is the one for you. I just don't want you to blow it."

"I'm not blowing anything." *She's the one who keeps turning me down.*

"Oh, I know *that* voice. It's your 'I'm the boss and you're not' voice."

He breathed deep and grumbled, "Lucy. Cut it out."

And she relented. "Okay. Just, you know, try to be open, will you?"

"Open. Absolutely. I will."

"Ha. I love you, Noah."

"Good. Be safe. Don't overdo it."

"I will be fine. I promise. Bye, now."

And she was gone. He set down the phone and thought of all the things he hadn't said: *Watch your back. Hold on to your purse. Stay out of dark alleyways. Set up those first appointments with your new doctors....*

He had so much advice he needed to give her. But she was on her own now. All grown up. And a continent away.

Alice didn't know what to do. Noah was shutting down on her, shutting her out. Whenever she tried to talk to him about it, he denied and evaded.

Maybe he was right. A little time apart wouldn't hurt them. It might do them good.

Or it might just be the simplest way to end it. She would go home; he would fly to Texas on business.

The days would go by, the weeks and the months. Somehow they would never quite get back together again....

She left for Montedoro Wednesday morning.

Noah kissed her goodbye at the front door. "Have a good trip," he said. Nothing else. No urging her to hurry back, not a single word about how much he would miss her or when he might come to her.

His coolness hurt. She longed to tell him she loved him, but she'd promised she wouldn't—not until she was ready to marry him. And how could she be ready when he wouldn't even talk to her about the things that really mattered?

So she kissed him back and whispered, "Take care."

Altus held open the car door and she got in.

And that was that. They drove away.

Noah returned from Texas on Friday. He'd sunk a big chunk of change into Yellow Rose Wind and Solar. And he had complete confidence in his decision to go in and go big.

There were other things he wasn't so confident about. Things like his sister's continued good health and well-being now she'd run off to New York to become a star in the fashion world. And Alice.

Alice most of all.

She'd left him without saying when she'd be back. He was pretty damn furious at her for that.

True, he hadn't *asked* when she would be back. He

hadn't offered to join her in Montedoro. But he felt justified in that. After all, *she* was the one leaving *him*. She should be the one to say when she planned to return.

And she hadn't called or emailed or texted him, either.

Well, all right. One text. To tell him she'd arrived home safely:

@ Nice Airport. Flt smooth. Njoy Texas.

He'd texted back, Thnx, a real conversation stopper. Because he didn't really want to text Alice.

Or talk to her on the phone.

Or correspond via email.

He wanted her with him, where he could touch her and see her smile. He wanted his ring on her finger and her sweet, strong body next to him in bed.

Wanted all that. And wanted it way, way too much.

So much it scared the crap out of him. So much it had him all upside down and turned around inside.

It wasn't supposed to be like this. She was supposed to say yes when he asked her—or at least, if she didn't say yes, he should be able to take it in stride. Patience and persistence were everything. He knew that. You kept your eye on the prize and you never gave up no matter what went down.

He was blowing it. He got that. Blowing it and determined to keep on blowing it.

It made no sense. *He* made no sense.

He was ashamed of himself and pissed off at her. And so lonely for her it made his bones ache.

Saturday, he called Lucy just to see how she was doing. And to give her all the important advice he hadn't managed to impart when she'd called the previous Monday. She chattered away, laughing, sharing way more information about her new life in New York City than he ever needed to know.

And he simply listened. And found himself smiling and nodding and now and then making an encouraging sound. He never did give her all that advice he'd been so anxious to share.

Because he realized she didn't need to hear it.

Somewhere around the time she started detailing how Mrs. Nichols across the landing had invited her over and they'd made cookies together—spice cookies with cinnamon and nutmeg and sugar sprinkled on top—the truth came to him.

Lucy was okay.

Lucy was going to be fine.

If she needed him, she would call him. For now, he'd done all he could for her.

It was her turn to soar, and he really couldn't help her with that.

He was just feeling kind of good for the first time in a week when she asked him about Alice. He didn't know what to say so he answered in single syllables, and she knew immediately that things weren't right. When she found out that Alice had gone to Montedoro and Noah had no idea when she'd be back, Lucy got all over him, calling him his own worst enemy, demanding to know if he'd lost his mind.

Noah let her rant on. What could he say? She was right after all.

When she finally wound down, she pleaded softly, "Go after her, Noah. Do not let her get away."

After that conversation, he felt worse than ever. He

went out to the stables and spent the day with his horses. It helped a little.

But not enough.

Monday, Orion arrived from the farm in Maryland. God, he was beautiful. To see that incredible iridescent coat shining in the California sun, well, that was something. Noah called in the vet to check him over. The vet declared him in excellent health. After the vet visit, Noah tacked him up and rode him. Orion amazed him, so calm and responsive for a stallion, especially a super-sensitive Teke recently cooped up in a trailer for the long ride from Maryland.

He started to whip out his phone and text Alice, just to let her know that Orion had finally arrived safe and well, to give her a hard time for parting with such an amazing animal.

But he didn't call.

What if she didn't answer? He had no idea where he stood with her now.

It had been five days since she'd left him. In some ways, those five days seemed a century. Or maybe two.

That got him feeling down all over again.

Back at the house, he showered and changed and then went down for a drink before dinner. He poured himself a double and drank it, staring out over the equestrian fields. When the glass was empty, he poured another.

Hannah served him his solitary dinner on the loggia.

He sat down and looked at the excellent meal she'd put in front of him and decided he wasn't hungry after all. "Hannah, another drink." He held up his glass to her.

She gave him one of those looks and said, "If you want to get wasted, you can do that on your own." And then she spun on her heel and marched back into the house.

He sat there for a moment after she left, fuming. And then he went after her.

"What the hell, Hannah?" he demanded when he got to the jut of white stone counter that separated the kitchen from the family room. He slammed the heavy crystal glass down. "What is your problem?"

Okay, he shouldn't have asked. He knew that. You didn't ask Hannah Russo what her problem was unless you wanted an earful.

"You," she said low, with a cold curl of her lip. "*You* are my problem, Noah. You, moping around here like someone did you wrong when we all know very well that *you're* the one in the wrong here."

"Now, you wait just a minute here…"

"No. Uh-uh. *You* wait, Noah. When are you going to wake up? You think I can't tell what's happened in this house? You think I don't know that you went out and found yourself the woman of your dreams and then brought her home only to send her away again?"

"I didn't—"

Hannah cut him off with a wave of her hand. "Don't even bother lying to me. I've known you for too long. I know what you're up to. You had some grandiose scheme to get yourself the ultimate trophy wife."

"What the… How did you—"

"*You* told me."

"I didn't—"

"You did. Maybe you didn't know that you did. But you told me all about her, including that she's a Montedoran princess. You said you were going to marry her, and that was before you even met her. I can add two and two and come up with four every time—and where was I? Oh, yeah. You went out to catch yourself a princess and instead you found someone to love you. Someone you love right back. That scares you. Love scares you. Well, you know what? You're not the least special. Everybody's scared. Everybody's afraid that they'll lose what they love the most. Everybody's afraid that they'll end up alone."

"I'm not—"

That time, she slapped her palm flat to the counter for silence. The sound echoed like a shot. "Yes, you *are*. You are afraid. And you are taking yourself way too seriously. You need to get over yourself. And here's a hot flash. Getting snockered on thirty-four-year-old Scotch is not going to give you anything but a headache in the morning. You need to go after her. You need to suck it up and say what's in your heart, Noah. You need to get down on your knees in front of her. You need to tell that sweet girl that you love her. You need to do it right away. Before she does exactly what you're afraid she'll do— which is to decide that you're not worth waiting for."

Chapter Thirteen

Alice was doing her best just making it through one day after another.

In some ways it was good to be back in Montedoro. To share long lunches with Rhia, to spend time with her horses.

The Autumn Faire came and went. She rode Yazzy in the parade wearing traditional Montedoran dress: full pink skirt with black trim, a frothy white blouse, a snug black vest embroidered with twining flowers and a round, flat, wide-brimmed hat with a black ribbon that tied beneath her chin. White tights and flat black shoes completed the ensemble.

Alice waved and smiled at the crowds that lined the narrow streets. A lot of people had cameras pressed against their faces or took pictures with their phones as she rode by. Alice just kept smiling even though she felt vaguely ridiculous. She knew she would end up all over the tabloids looking like a country milkmaid.

Which was fine, she reminded herself. Looking like a milkmaid was a significant improvement over coming off like a refugee from an episode of *Girls Behaving Badly*.

After the parade, she went home to change. Dami showed up and coaxed her out for a coffee with him. They sat in a favorite café and he told her what a delight

Lucy was and then asked her why Noah hadn't come with her for the Faire.

She sipped her espresso and said she didn't want to talk about Noah.

And Dami surprised her by not pressing her to say more. He took her hand and kissed the back of it, and then turned it over and pretended to see her future in her palm. "Great happiness. True love. Horses. Children— lots and lots of children." He faked a look of dismay. "Far too many of them, if you ask me."

She eased her hand away. "You just never know, Dami."

He didn't lose his beautiful smile. "Perhaps *you* don't. But *I* know. You are a ray of boldly shining light in a world that is too often boring and gray. You were born to be happy. And you will be. Just watch."

Alice hoped her charming brother might be right. But as each day went by, she grew more afraid that if there was to be happiness for her, it wouldn't be with Noah.

Michelle clucked over her and whipped up delicious meals to tempt her flagging appetite. Alice ate the wonderful food without much pleasure. Everything seemed gray and sad to her, even Michelle's excellent cooking.

More than once she considered simply hopping a flight and returning to California. But she didn't do it— which was unlike her. She'd always been one to go after what she wanted.

With Noah, though…

It just didn't feel right to go running after him. He'd sent her away alone, though she'd asked him twice to come with her. He wanted her to marry him, but he wouldn't or couldn't say that he loved her. He didn't even seem to want her to say that *she* loved him. It was all too perplexing, and she didn't know what to do about it, didn't know how to get through to him.

So she did nothing.

Rhia gave her a hard time about that. "Waiting. That's what you're doing. You realize that, don't you? Waiting for him to make the first move. It's so…backward of you to wait for a man to make the moves. That's just not you, Allie. You're a woman of action. And you need to go to him, work things out with him, together, the two of you…."

Maybe Rhia was right.

But deep in her heart, Alice didn't think so. Alice thought that Noah needed time to figure a few things out.

She was giving him that time.

At least that was what she told herself.

While she waited.

And did nothing.

Thank God for her horses. Without them, it all would have been too much to bear. She gave her days to them gratefully, rising long before daylight to be the first one at the stables, not going back to her villa until sunset.

On the last Wednesday in October, she woke from her restless dreams even earlier than usual. She went straight to the stables and tacked up the chestnut mare Rosanna to ride. She'd just set the saddle well forward on the mare's fine back when she heard it: the soft rhythmic rustling of a broom brushing the floor.

Her heart roaring in her ears and her gloved hands suddenly trembling, she turned.

He was there at the edge of the shadows, tall, strong, golden. Wearing battered jeans, an old sweatshirt and worn Western boots.

His name filled up her throat. She hesitated to let it

out, struck silent by the absurd certainty that he was only a fantasy brought on by her own desperation and longing, that he would vanish as soon as she dared to acknowledge him with sound.

She made herself say his name anyway. "Noah?"

He dropped the broom. It clapped and clattered against the stone floor. And then he was lifting his head to face her. He tried on a smile that didn't quite make it. In those blue eyes she saw hope and fear and so many sweet, tender questions.

And love.

She did. At last. She saw his love.

He made a noise, a tight, tortured sound. And in a whisper, he said, "Alice." He held out his arms.

It was enough. It was everything.

With a soft cry, she covered the distance between them in swift strides. He scooped her up and she grabbed on tight.

He turned them in a circle there in the darkened stable, so early in the morning it still felt like night. His cheek, rough with morning stubble, pressed to hers—at first.

And then he turned his head just that little bit more. Their lips met in a kiss that told her all the things she needed so desperately to know. A kiss that promised tomorrow.

And the next day.

And all the days after that.

On Friday they flew to Los Angeles.

They took a suite at the Beverly Hills Hotel and made love for hours. When they finally fell asleep, exhausted from jet lag, pleasure and happiness, they slept until the middle of the following day.

At three in the afternoon, they stood on a palm-tree-lined street in the pretty, hilly neighborhood of Silver Lake. He showed her the Spanish-style house that his parents had owned, where he'd lived until the money ran out after his father died.

"It's a comfortable house," he said. "Built in the 1920s and big for that era. Four bedrooms, two baths. A great house to raise a family."

She linked her arm with his and shaded her eyes with her other hand. "You loved it here."

He nodded, his gaze on the house where he used to live. "We were happy. Safe. Until my father died, I honestly thought no trouble could touch me—or maybe I didn't actually think it. It was simply true. A fact of life. But then one morning, he kissed my mother goodbye, walked out the front door and fell off a roof two hours later. Everything changed."

She leaned her head against his shoulder and wished she could think of something both helpful and profound to say. All that came was, "It's so sad. And scary…"

He tipped her chin up and kissed her, just a tender brush of his mouth across hers. "Come on."

They got back in the car and he told the driver where to go next.

Twenty minutes later the car pulled to the curb on another street, where the houses were smaller and more run-down, with barred windows and doors.

They got out and stood on the sidewalk by the car, beneath a beautiful tree with delicate fernlike leaves. "A jacaranda," she said. "We have them in Montedoro, too."

He pointed at the house across the street, a small stucco bungalow painted a truly awful shade of turquoise. The paint was peeling, the doors and windows barred. A battered chain-link fence marked off the tiny bare yard. "One bedroom," he said. "One bath. My mother slept on the sofa. Lucy had the bedroom. There was an extra room, very small, in the back. I had a cot in there. I hated that house. But not because it was so ugly and cramped. It just... It always felt empty to me. Empty and sad. Well, except for Lucy. She was like a bright ray of light, even when she was so sick and I was sure we would lose her like we lost my dad."

"So, then, it wasn't *all* bad."

"Bad enough," he said gruffly, still staring at the turquoise house.

She reached up and guided his face around to look at her. "It means so much to me that you've brought me here."

He turned to her fully then, there beneath the lacy branches of the jacaranda tree, and he gazed down at her steadily, his eyes like windows on the wide-open sky. "I love you, Alice." He said it softly but firmly, too. Without hesitation and with no equivocation. "You are my heart, my life, all the hope for the future I didn't even realize I was looking for. I want you to marry me, but if you're not ready, I swear I can be patient. I can wait as long as you need me to."

She put her hands on his chest, felt his heart beating strong and steady beneath her palm. "Oh, Noah..." Across the street, a woman with long black hair pushed a stroller in front of the house where Noah used to live. Two boys raced past in the middle of the street, laughing and bouncing a ball between them. She thought that it wasn't such a bad street, really, that there were people in the small houses around them who loved and cared for each other, who looked to the future with hope in their hearts. She whispered, "I was so afraid you wouldn't come to find me."

He laughed then, but it was a ragged, torn sort of sound. "Me, too." He took her by the shoulders and met her eyes again. "The love thing. Talking about it, saying it out loud… It's hard for me."

She laid her hand against his cheek. "It will get easier. Love is like that. The more you give, the more you have to give."

"Think so, huh?"

"I know so."

"Hannah got fed up with me," he confessed. "She told me off, said I was scared to love you and I'd better get over myself and deal with my fear before you got tired of waiting for me."

She shook her head and dared a smile. "It would have taken a long time for me to get that tired. But I'm glad you came sooner rather than later."

"I gave some thought to what Hannah said…"

"And?"

His mouth twisted wryly. "It's old news."

"Tell me anyway."

He glanced up into the ferny branches of the tree, then down at the cracked sidewalk and finally into her eyes again. "My parents, that's all."

"They made you afraid to love? But how? From all you've told me, they did love you, very much. And they loved each other.…"

He lifted a hand and stroked her hair, his touch so sure and steady—and cherishing, too. "I know. It doesn't make sense. They loved each other absolutely. Even I knew that, and I was only a kid. But my mother was never the same once he was gone. She let everything go.

She was like a ghost of herself. She was…just hanging around, waiting for it to be over."

"Oh, Noah. Are you sure? Did she say actually that?"

"No, of course not. But she didn't have to. It was there in her face all the time. That faraway look, a bottomless sort of sadness. The day we lost her, I think she knew what would happen if she didn't get to the doctor. But she wouldn't go. She wanted to be with my dad. It was where she'd wanted to be all along."

Alice started to speak.

He put his finger against her lips. "I realize I'll never know for certain that she let herself die. I realize she did the best she could and that we survived, Lucy and me."

"But you've been afraid. Afraid to love so much…"

He nodded. And then he bent and he kissed her. It was the sweetest kiss, tender and slow.

When he lifted his head, she said, "Don't be afraid. Or if you are, do it anyway. Love me anyway."

"I will," he replied. "I do."

And then, slowly and clearly, she said, "Yes, Noah. I will marry you."

He looked so startled she almost laughed. And then he demanded, "You mean it? You will?"

"I love you. And yes. I will."

He stuck his hand into his pocket and came out with the ring he'd offered her that first time they made love. When she shook her head in wonderment, he explained, "I've been carrying it around with me all along, just in case. It got to be like a talisman. I kept it on me even after you left California."

"Noah, I do believe you're a complete romantic."

"Shh. Don't tell anyone. Let it be our secret."

She gave him her hand and he slipped it on her finger. It was a perfect fit. "I love it," she whispered. "I love *you*."

They shared another slow and tender kiss.

Then, hand in hand, they turned for the waiting car.

* * * * *

Watch for Damien and Lucy's story,
HOLIDAY ROYALE,
coming in December 2013,
only from Harlequin Special Edition.